Hollywood Psycho

The Luke Townsend Story

Brittany Roth

ISBN: 979-8-9881300-2-4

ISBN (ebook): 979-8-9881300-3-1

www.brittrothauthor.com

Cover design by Lopes Designs

Interior and formatting by Michael Davie

To the friends I've made. Thank you for believing in me. You know who you are.
Thank you.

Dear Reader

Dear Reader,

I hope this note finds you well and in positive spirits. Although this book may not go into extensively graphic detail in certain scenes, it does touch base on some topics that may be triggers for some.

In Luke's story, we have a woman who suffers abuse mentally and physically by the hand of her domestic partner. She is raped and forced to perform oral acts.

This story also has elements of catfishing, talks about a miscarriage (not in detail, just says that there was one) and does have a murder scene. These scenes do not go into intense detail, but they are there.

If any of these topics stir up unwanted feelings, then I ask you to please not read this story. I want you to be happy and enjoy a book because reading is something you love to do. I do not want to bring about past or present memories you do not want to relive.

If you are in a situation where you need assistance, here are some resources I hope can help. I am also always here to listen or help in any way I can

Emergency Services:
911
National Domestic Violence Hotline (24/7):
(800) 799-7233
Text BEGIN to 88788
www.thehotline.org
National Sexual Assault Hotline (24/7):
(800) 656-4673
www.RAINN.org
988 Suicide and Crisis Lifeline (24/7):
988
Text 988
www.988lifeline.org

With Love,
Brittany Roth

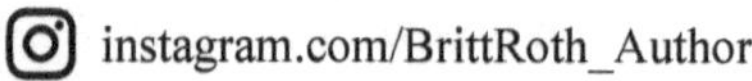 instagram.com/BrittRoth_Author
 tiktok.com/@BrittRoth_Author

Chapter One

I've lived a privileged life, of which, I am aware. I could end my story here, because not very many people may be interested in it. But even though I've lived a life far different than the majority of the world, I'm lucky enough to still be here *with* my story. With lessons that may help people who have ever been in the situation that I once naïvely found myself in. It all begins with my backstory and, like I said, the privileged life I lived. My parents, Orson and Carter Townsend, were artists who found themselves thriving in the New York art scene during the eighties, when revolutionary art took hold and made it one gigantic party after another. My parents were photographers who had an eye for the human form. They shot photographs of their peers working on their art, people working on the streets, people who were constantly creating. Their images became a staple amongst well-renowned artists, movie stars, singers, even the political elites. They all came together to cherish what my parents had the eye to create. What they had the eyes to see.

Their friends were great inspirations to them and came from all walks of life. But their true inspiration came from the ones more overlooked; the starving artists, like they once were. Those were the people who made their mark on my parents' hearts and inspired their art to succeed to endless limits. They showed the truth behind human form.

When the mid-nineties came around and the art scene changed, they decided to create their final piece of art. They would say it was their greatest work to date. *Me.*

After I was born, they began their new journey of curating shows for unknown artists, which inevitably catapulted them to the top of the new and accepted art scene. There were endless parties full of everyone my parents loved and adored, who loved and adored them back. But the fulfillment New York once gave them didn't feel right for raising a child, so they made the move to Beverly Hills to give me a more "normal" upbringing. But my life has been anything but normal.

My name is Luke Townsend, named after the man who bought my parents' first photograph. I know I have what would traditionally be considered more of a masculine name, but my parents had unique names of their own for their time. Growing up, I could say that I got made fun of for the name I was given, but that would be a lie. I was rarely ever in school with peers my own age. Instead, I was living coast to coast with my parents, very much different from the life they envisioned.

Instead of being in traditional school, I could always be found sitting in a corner somewhere, during a show, with only my parents' adult friends to talk to. I do, however, give the utmost praise, respect, and admiration to my tutor, Isabelle, who introduced me to reading and my love of the written word.

Different worlds consumed me, because I was living in one where I didn't quite fit in. Characters became my friends and even family at times. They were always there, and I could go wherever and become whoever I wanted each and every time I picked up a book.

Isabelle even introduced me to the classics. She said they were important because they set a standard of literary importance. But reading anything, any genre, was important because there were people all over the world writing these stories that came from their imagination and would only broaden mine.

When I hit puberty, everything changed. I blossomed, as my mother would say. Really, I'd just grown into my features. I was tall, thin, and would be considered a natural beauty.

Artists at my parents' parties began to take notice of me. They wanted *me* to be their muse. There I was, my parents' greatest creation, finally out in the world for people to see. I was their real life photograph, and everyone took notice. I started to get invited, personally, to fashion shows all over the world and parties I had no business attending. People just wanted to say that Luke Townsend had been there. Now, don't get me wrong, I loved every second of it. But I missed who I really was; my true nature, if you will. I missed the invisible little girl who could sit in a corner and read for hours upon hours, getting lost in her own imagination and feeling seen in a world no one else could see.

On my seventeenth birthday, I finally found it in me to ask my parents if I could attend an actual school to finish out my senior year. Even though I could've gotten my diploma two years prior thanks to Isabelle, I wanted to feel grounded, like I was living the life of "normalcy" my parents thought I had. Without question, they agreed.

On my first day at a private school near our Beverly Hills home, I went in with the intention of making friends. I wanted to be someone who was liked. I wanted to be seen as a real person and not just who they saw on magazine covers or read articles about. I wanted to be like everyone else. I wanted to talk about the same things; clothes, music, boys. I wanted to be ordinary. But the kids at my school were anything but. They only cared about labels, what cars they had to drive, and about who they knew and had partied with the night before.

I had nearly accepted that I had made a mistake in deciding to attend a school when I heard a voice from behind me. "Hey, you're the new girl. That's cool. Wanna hang out at lunch?"

In that brief moment I thought, 'Why did I want to be ordinary when I had every opportunity possible to be extraordinary?' So, in the split second of that thought I decided I would reinvent myself and be who everyone thought I was. I would become Luke Townsend, the "It" girl. The party girl. The fashion girl. The muse.

"Yeah, I'd love to," I answered, turning around to meet the eyes of Margot Spencer, the real "It" girl of our school.

"Cool. I'm Margot. This is Franklin and Remy," she said, pointing to two guys sitting in desks beside her.

"Hi, I'm Luke."

"Yeah, we know," Remy said.

"So, what's it like taking over my spot as the most popular girl in school?"

"Umm, hadn't thought about it. Sorry, I guess," I flipped back around.

"I'm just kidding. But I do want to know why you never kept in touch over the years."

I whipped back around, confused. "What do you mean?"

"Oh, she doesn't remember us," she said, looking to Franklin, then to Remy.

Franklin pouted his lips. "That's sad."

My brow arched, thinking they were mistaken. I had never met them before; I had never met *anyone* before.

"We were your only friends in Kindergarten for the three weeks you were there." Margot exchanged a knowing look between Remy and Franklin, an amused smile on her face.

I had a vague memory of that. But honestly, I'd completely forgotten I'd even attended a real school until that moment. I wanted friends. I wanted a life with normal—well, as normal as they could be—experiences like I had read in every single book I consumed. So, I faked it.

"Oh my god! Yes! Margot, Franklin, and Remy! I almost forgot. I'm so sorry. How could I have ever forgotten you guys? I've thought about you guys so much over the years and missed you. I've wanted to reach out but have always been on the go with my parents." I paused. "You know, they can never stay in the same place for too long. Always back and forth. It's a lot." I smiled, happy with my answer.

"See, I told you she'd remember us, Margot," Remy winked.

Margot brushed it off as if I were telling the truth, although she knew I wasn't. I *had* forgotten them.

That first day, getting reacquainted with my once-upon-a-time "friend group," was the best first day I could've hoped for. We spent every second together after that. We were inseparable. We could always be seen shopping, going out to eat, going to the movies. We were social. We were at every party and barely scathing by in school. Even though education was important to me, I dialed back my knowledge to fit in. I just wanted them to feel like I was actually one of them, because I was. I was just another teenager, wanting to be young and to have fun.

During that time of adolescence, it didn't matter whose house we went to. We were all basically raising ourselves with no one truly looking out for us. We raised each other. Then it came time to graduate, and that within itself felt unreal. It felt like I had accomplished something more in life. Not just a sacred rite of passage every normal teenager gets to experience. It was something personal to me because it was the first time I had made a huge milestone with my peers. But to Margot, Remy, and Franklin, it meant we were even more free.

They were right. We didn't have to show up to a place we were forced to be at anymore. I mean, I never had that until I started attending a physical school, but for the short time I was there, it was suffocating not being able to do whatever I wanted every day. I'm sure you can imagine or have experienced it yourself. Truly, I didn't mind it though, because I was there for the social aspect of it. I'm sure that's what the majority of people feel. I guess in a sense, I did get the experience I was seeking.

We didn't go on to college and further our educations. We didn't need to. We had our absent parents funding our lifestyles and we didn't want it any other way. It also didn't seem like they cared either. Of course, because I grew up always with my parents, we were very close. I know it sounds like they didn't care because of how I described my life then, but they did. I just wanted to be like my friends. So, I got used to pretending like they didn't pay attention to me.

My parents were quite the opposite, actually. We spent a lot of time together. Too much time, probably. They loved me very much and I loved them. I still do, very much, to this day. Because I was their greatest creation, they took a lot of time, effort, and love into making *me* be great.

We talked about world events. What I enjoyed reading, art and history, etc. They taught me how to help others and how to look for the good in people, even if it didn't seem like any was there, but how looking a bit harder would usually reveal a little piece of good in them.

They made me feel like I was more of a friend than a child, but still very much loved. They made me well rounded and wise beyond my years, which is something I don't take for granted.

Amongst our constant travelling, they made sure that at every stop we went to museums and exhibitions. I would then have to write a paper about what I learned and turn it in to them by the next day. I found those papers recently and shed a tear of happiness with how much my parents cared about me. They were the only two people I really knew. The parties were only a chunk of hours in my life where I wasn't their constant fixation. The three of us had an incredible bond, something I will cherish for the rest of my life and maybe, one day, pass along to my own child.

Back to my story, though. Partying became a significant part of our lives after high school. I never did drugs. I was never even tempted to try. I would have the occasional glass of champagne, though. It was the only time I had ever felt like I was living dangerously. I was living on the edge, if you will. Going out constantly led me to meeting the first boy I was ever in love with, Richie. He was the lead singer of an up-and-coming band in L.A., and was definitely *not* what people thought I would normally go after, seeing as I was the 'snooty rich girl' from Beverly Hills.

Richie was the bad boy I fantasized about and secretly longed for my entire life. He was my Heathcliff, my Dorian Gray, my Ponyboy, my Damon Salvatore. He was the bad boy who made it feel even more exciting to love, almost as if it were . . . . . . forbidden. Richie was the first real life boy I'd ever had a crush on. The first real life boy I actually fell in love with. He was the one who made it seem like the whole world was going to be ours, forever. Like nothing could ever come between us. We were destined to be together.

It warms my heart now thinking about him and how when we were so madly in love at nineteen. Feeling like we'd discovered the greatest thing in the world, each other, which was a rush unlike anything I'd ever felt before. It was a love so new to my heart. So pure. So true. So innocent. It didn't seem like it would ever end. We were always together. I was always his number one supporter and biggest fan. And then he became my first, the one I gave my whole self to.

We talked about running away together, just being the two of us. We dreamed, like any young couple would, of starting a family and living the life we'd always wanted for ourselves. We had that in common. Richie was my constant and he quickly became my, *everything*.

Then Richie gave me the gift of falling in love with the second love of my life. The most *indescribable* love of my life. A love only the two of you will ever know because you're the only two who know what each other's hearts feel like from the inside. That love, that indescribable love was my Lily who I only knew for five months before I lost her. The love I had for her was an all-consuming love that made me want to keep going even though I was in the darkest place I'd ever been before. It was a love I didn't know existed until I experienced it, and it opened my eyes to what I could actually do in this world, how I could actually make a difference.

Richie did the honest thing, as he said, and proposed to me when we found out. We were elated and couldn't wait to start living the dream we had talked about. But once the dream was lost and we were in heartache, Richie became, not so honest, and he left me for someone else. That's when I realized the world could be very two sided and people aren't always who they could appear to be.

Margot, Franklin and Remy embraced me back under their wings, nursing me back to whatever image of myself I had before the treacherous heartache I was left in. But that wasn't what I wanted for myself any longer. I wanted more. I *needed* more. I wanted to take whatever this life had, because it had taken so much from me already. So, I reinvented myself once again with the new and improved Luke Townsend, socialite, who was unlucky to fall in love with the third and greatest love of my life. The unlucky love of my life who this story, this *terrible* story, is about.

Chapter Two

I sucked up whatever emotions I had about the greatest loss in my life and shoved it down to a place I refused to ever open again. I took the world head on, paving my way even higher to the top, securing myself as the girl everyone couldn't *wait* to see or read about in the papers. Whether it was good or bad, I didn't care.

Fortunately, I was still sought after by designers who couldn't *wait* to dress me in the hopes of having their clothes photographed by paparazzi. Making the average person, I apologize for lack of a better term, do whatever they could to get their hands on their clothing, purses, accessories, you name it. I wasn't just the "it" girl, I was "the" girl, and everyone wanted a piece of me.

Beverly Hills had been my permanent home since I was seventeen, but now being twenty-one, I began to jet set from coast to coast once more, staying at our New York apartment, house in The Hamptons, or with friends I was beginning to get close to in Paris, London and even Japan. I wanted my face out there. I took every opportunity thrown at me to get whatever recognition I could to further numb the pain I had inside. Margot, Franklin and Remy were always in tow, as if to be my . . . . . . entourage. They didn't have anything else going on in their lives and this was the life they wanted to live. So, I let them tag along. But really, it was for me. I loved the familiar companionship, and they made it not so lonely.

I didn't spiral out of control, like I know people hoped I would, because being in control was what I knew was going to make me succeed. I did, however, let myself indulge. Once a month, I'd allow myself a few extra glasses of champagne to really loosen up. The rest of the time, I was faking being drunk to get stories spun about "It Girl Luke Townsend Trashed at Club." "Posh or Pissed?" "Luke Townsend: A Wasted Wreck." I had to give the people a little something every once in a while, to keep them wanting more.

What drove the tabloids crazy was how I would never let anyone see me with a man. Ever. That would change every-thing because it would mean Luke Townsend either had "calmed down" or was possibly ready to "settle down." And at that time in my life, I wasn't sure if I was ready for that. I didn't want to get hurt again.

I did see men though. I saw a lot of them, actually. Not too many, but if the media saw how many I was with, whether it be a high or low number, they would probably say I was running through men faster than you could change a shirt, or plainly just refer to me as a slut. I didn't want that label put upon myself. So, I would have private, secret if you will, rendezvous with men I found attractive. They were sworn to secrecy not to tell anyone. I went as far as having them sign NDA's. All of that made the allure of Luke Townsend, the creation, even more of a prize, a trophy, a chase, for men who wanted me.

Margot on the other hand didn't have a reputation to uphold. She was just along for the ride. "Do you think I can get him to buy me underwear?"

"Oh God Margot, only *you* would ask that." Remy's dramatic eye roll made me let out a giggle.

"What?! I don't feel like going home tonight. And besides, you can tell a lot about a man on whether or not he'll buy you underwear."

"Umm, how exactly?" Franklin's brow raised, curious to hear her answer.

I think we all were curious to hear what delusion Margot would conjure up to justify never wanting to go home while we were out.

"Maybe we should cut you off." Remy pulled her glass away just as it was about to touch her lips. "I think the bubbles are getting to your head."

"Well, if he agrees to buy me underwear, he's one of two types of men. The first being he just wants to sleep with me. The second, he's the type of man who wants to take care of me which makes *me* want to sleep with *him*. So, it's a win-win for me either way."

"But how do you tell the difference?" I asked her smugly.

She looked up in wonder as the lights flashed around the club, music and smoke filling the air, looking like a child lost in a daydream only she could pull herself out from. "I guess I just . . . . . . decide which one they are. It never goes past that night anyways," she shrugged.

"Margot, you're . . ." Franklin started.

"What? Innovative? Fresh? Tell me Franklin, what am I?"

He narrowed his eyes, smacking his lips. "Eccentric. But in a good way." He rested his hand gently over her knee.

"I think we should all be more like Luke." Remy nodded my way.

"And how's that?" Margot shifted, cocking her head towards him.

"Discrete."

"There's just a time and a place, that's all." I shrugged, and the subject was dropped. They always knew when I wanted to change the topic. That's definitely a quality in each of them I enjoyed. We could have all the fun in the world, but once a fleeting moment was over, each one of us knew it. We never dwelled on it or let it go beyond what it was, just a moment.

We were usually in a new city each week. Mostly because it was exciting always being in a new place. It made the never settling down portion of my image permanent. People wanted to see where I would end up each week and I wanted to see the ridiculous headline made up about me.

After a while, I started to notice a man I had recognized from a few times before. He was always alone. He was always standing in a corner or up on a landing where he appeared to be overseeing everything. Like he was just watching. Observing.

I soon began to notice that he wasn't just looking at anything specific. He would be looking at *me*. Not always, but when I would get that funny feeling, like someone's staring at you, sure enough, when I would look around, there he would be in his overseeing position. Eyes on me, and not taking them off.

He was handsome and alluring. Seductive, even, in a way only an attractive stranger could be. Well, one you couldn't stop thinking about. That's the effect he had on me, and that effect didn't come often. I hadn't been this attracted to a man since Richie. Although I was attracted to the men I spent evenings with, it never felt like this. Like I wanted to pursue something. They were just cute little place fillers until the real thing came along.

～

One night when we were back home in L.A., I noticed him once again. "Who is that guy?" I yelled into Remy's ear.

"I have no idea, but he's fucking sexy," he yelled back.

"He hasn't taken his eyes off me all night. Actually, every night I've seen him," I leaned closer to Remy. "He was at the club last week in Miami and the week before in New York. Should I go talk to him?"

Remy placed his hand to his chest as if offended by my question. "HELL NO!! If he wants you, he needs to make the move."

"Yeah, but I just want to know why I keep seeing him everywhere."

"We do drink massive amounts of champagne, maybe you're having a Margot moment and just *think* he looks like someone you saw. And besides, even if he is the same guy, you're Luke *Fucking* Townsend. Men chase *you*, not the other way around." he quipped.

"You're right." I kept staring back at my handsome stranger curious to find out who this mysterious man was. He was intriguing and that made it hard not to think about him. I wondered who he was. I wondered when and where I would see him next. It almost started to become a game. And before I knew it, I realized that I didn't just want to see him to find out why he was always there staring at me, I wanted to know him. I wanted to know why I found him so attractive, and not in my usual one-night kind of way. He had become someone I wanted to pursue. Someone I could incorporate into my reinvention. Someone I thought I could love.

A lost, familiar feeling of my heart racing started to happen whenever I saw him. That feeling lead to an anticipation of whether or not it would be the night we would speak. He was the one thing in my life I couldn't control. I *tried* not to think about him, but every time I stepped foot anywhere, whether it be a plane, a restaurant, even shopping, I was always looking for him. Trying to see if I could spot the eyes of the one I knew was for me. Looking to see if he was there amongst the faces of passer-byers with his eyes only on me. I wanted to see his handsome face. His intriguing eyes. The shape of his lips. I had only ever seen him from a distance. I didn't even know what color those intriguing eyes were. I just knew they were burned into me and kept me wanting more. This man, this sexy, seductive man who was a familiar stranger had taken hold of every part of my mind. And yet, I couldn't allow myself to approach because like Remy had said, I was Luke "Fucking" Townsend and men pursued *me*. I wasn't going to let the facade of this girl I created be ruined for something I knew wouldn't just be one night.

"There he is again, over by the bar." I leaned into Remy, pointing to my mystery man while sitting sideline at a polo match.

"Who?" He looked, trying to place someone, yet not recognizing anyone.

"The guy I keep seeing everywhere. He's standing by the bar."

"Okay, this is getting a little creepy. Maybe he's a stalker."

"Who has a stalker?" Franklin interrupted, sitting down next to me.

"Luke does."

"Oh, of course she does. Where is he?"

"By the bar. Blue suit." I motioned with my glass.

"Oh, he's sexy."

"That's what I said the first time I saw him," Remy exaggerated, smacking the table glancing towards Franklin.

"How many times have you seen him?" Margot decided to pipe up in the midst of taking photos of herself.

"I first noticed him in New York, and I've seen him almost every weekend since," I paused. "Should I be worried? Or does he seem harmless? I mean . . . . . . look at him." I took a sip of champagne playing it off as if he was someone of no importance or value all while longing for him to approach me.

"Well, if he's getting into these kinds of events, I'd say he's harmless," she shrugged, making a pouting expression for another photo.

"I was very intrigued at first because I do find him a little attractive. But now, showing up *here*, at this private event, I don't really know what to think." I said.

"And rightfully so," Franklin remarked. "Have you tried talking to him yet? Maybe ask him why he's following you around?"

"Remy told me not to."

"We don't pursue men, they pursue us," he said, adamantly.

"Very true," Franklin agreed. "Well, I guess just keep seeing if he keeps showing up. Or make it more easily accessible to access you. Maybe he's intimated to talk to you. Some men are *dreadfully* intimidated by a beautiful woman."

"Hmm, I'll think about it." That was the best advice I'd been given for this situation. I was too blinded by the mystery of him that I wasn't thinking clearly. Having a stalker never crossed my mind either. I was prepared to fall in love, not to never be found.

It all gave more speculation as to who he was and the thrill of chasing after what his intentions with me might be. Even though my life around that time was full of constant parties and travel, it was starting to grow boring. Having something unexpected in the form of a handsome man gave it a new little spark to keep things interesting.

"I'll be right back; I'm going to the ladies room." I excused myself and left our seats.

I checked my face and reapplied my lipstick in the mirror before heading to the bar. I was hoping to see him up close so I could see if his distant face matched what I imagined it looked like up close.

"Pardon me," a deep, rustic, yet soothing voice said to me as we collided into one another.

When I looked up, I was met with the eyes that had been burned into me.

"It was my fault, I apologize."

"Nothing could ever be a beautiful woman's fault," he replied keeping his eyes on mine.

This was the moment I had waited for, for *weeks*. He was here, directly in front of me and even more handsome than I thought he was. All I could do was smile. My invented self never shied away from words I didn't always need to use them but was never afraid to do so. Yet, this man had me speechless. Frozen before him where everything suddenly became a blur. Except for him. He was the only one I could see. Everything and everyone around us somehow disappeared.

Then he spoke the three little words that captivated me in a way where I knew everything was about to change. *I was about to change.*

"Hi, I'm Mitch."

Chapter Three

Mitch Bellamy. The man of my dreams. The man I knew I was going to spend the rest of my life with the second I first saw him staring at me weeks prior. You hear a lot, or read a lot, about love at first sight. It all seems too good to be true. A fairytale. But when it does happen to someone, like it happened to me in real life, it's an all-consuming burst of love. It's a feeling like you're home. Content. Happy. There's nothing like it in the world and I've experienced a lot of things within my privileged life. But having that instant attraction to someone you don't even know, yet feeling like you already know everything about them, is such a wonderful, complete feeling. It's rather inde-scribable. It's a feeling of knowing. Knowing that you found, *the one*.

"Hello, I'm Luke."

"Luke, that's an interesting name for such a beautiful woman."

I smiled, feeling the pounding of my heart beating in my chest. "I'm named after a very special person in my family's life. Someone we think about and celebrate often."

"Well then, who am I to say anything about it? It's a special name fit for a special woman."

"And how do you know I'm so special?"

"Because I haven't been able to keep my eyes off of you."

The blood rushed to my cheeks, burning them from the inside out. Richie was the only other man in my life to ever make me feel like I was something more than who the world thought I was. Yet here, before me, was this man, Mitch, who I'd instantly fallen for, telling me things any woman would love to hear. This reinvented version of myself who I swore would never let this happen to, had broken. And she was now being led by her heart instead of her head.

"I don't mean to be forward, but have you been stalking me?" I asked.

He let out a slight laugh. "Excuse me?" He grinned, in the cutest way, from the right side of his mouth.

"Yes, I feel like I've seen you before. I know I have. For weeks now, actually. I feel like I've been seeing you every-where I turn."

He stood there continuing to smile at me in a way only an attractive man could. "Well, I can't lie to a beautiful woman. You caught me. You *have* seen me a few times. And I know this, because I've seen you."

"So," I paused. "Why?"

"I invest in nightclubs. I travel around almost every week going to new clubs to see if I want to invest in their group. We're also currently looking to build a new club right here in L.A. It's what I do for a living."

My cheeks flushed with embarrassment. "Oh. That makes sense. I'm sorry if I offended you in any way. I've just . . . . . . seen you looking at me before and was curious as to who you were."

"There's no need to apologize. You're too beautiful for that."

I blushed again.

"I'm basically the overseer of the majority of the nightlife scene right now. I've turned run down places completely around. So, a lot of the owners like to get my opinions on what can elevate their club. A lot of the time they want me to make an investment in their establishments. My goal, like I said, is to open our own here in L.A. and hopefully branch out and create a string of nightlife entertainment facilities."

"Wow, that's sounds very exciting."

"It is. But I'll admit, at times it can very lonely. Always traveling around. Even though I work in the nightlife industry, it doesn't mean I have one." He leaned in, his lips nearing my ear. "You want to know a little secret?"

My breathing became heavy as his closeness invoked a yearning. "Okay."

"I'm the type of guy who would much rather settle down and start a family with a beautiful woman," he paused, slightly grazing my arm, sending goosebumps all over. "Every time I've seen you, I couldn't help but think how beautiful you were. That somehow, I had to know your name because one day I'd want to start a life with you. But I've always been too afraid to approach because what would a beautiful woman want with a man like me?"

The slow whispers of his voice sent my chest rising and falling with the intensity of a spark only someone you had an instant connection with could light. We'd never spoken before. We had no idea who either one of us were, but he was familiar. He made me feel comfortable in a way I'd only known once before. He made me love him even before I knew his name, and more so, after.

He pulled away from me. His lingering breath still warm on my skin.

"Well, I don't think I'm a very intimidating kind of woman."

"Oh, but that you are Luke. I'm not a man who has any trouble speaking to a beautiful woman. But with you, you have me in a grip I wouldn't even know how to get out of. To tell you the truth, I don't want to."

"How is that possible? We've only just met."

"Haven't you ever just known something was meant to be? Like you were in the right place at the right time? And how if you didn't take any action, you wouldn't be able to stop thinking about whatever it is you saw?" he paused. "Well, that was me, with you. I saw you and didn't do anything. I couldn't get your image out of my head, but I was lucky enough to see you again and again. It almost became a game for me, trying to find you amongst the sea of people and darkness every night. And even though I never said anything to you on those nights, when I saw you get up from your seat today, I knew that if I didn't take my shot, I probably never would. It was like the universe was pushing us to be together. So, to you, I apologize for bumping into you, *intentionally*."

It was like Mitch was reading my every thought. He knew how I felt. It was kismet. Destiny. He'd even said so himself.

Every ounce of caution went out the window. He was saying all the right things and then some. The Luke Townsend in that space of time knew she was changing. She was evolving. She was becoming the Luke Townsend she'd always wanted to be . . . Happy.

We walked back to my table where I introduced him to my friends. "Everyone this is Mitch. Mitch this is Margot, Franklin and Remy."

"It's nice to meet you all."

"So, is the stalker a friend or foe?" Remy questioned.

"I'd say friend, but hoping to be more." Mitch flashed his perfect smile, looking at me in a way that made me feel desired. "I didn't know I was already such a fixation amongst you all."

"Not really. This is the first time we've ever talked about you, actually." Margot retorted, not taking her eyes from her own reflection. "But we're glad you're not a stalker. That wouldn't be too good for our image."

"And what image would that be?" Mitch questioned.

The three of them looked towards Mitch as if they were appalled he even had to ask. "You really have no idea who Luke is, do you? Where she comes from?" Remy asked.

"No, I really don't. I've only seen her for the first time a few weeks ago. And I just found out her name a few moments ago. Only her first name actually," he answered.

Remy narrowed his eyes taking in my mysterious stranger turned eligible suitor. He and I were always closer to one another than Franklin or Margot ever were to me. He had a protective nature about him which made me feel closer to him than the others and I felt safe which made it easier to trust him completely. Maybe more than I'd ever trusted anyone else, except for Richie. "Well, it's Townsend."

"As in?" Mitch lingered, waiting for one of my friends to answer. But they didn't. "Should I know what that's supposed to mean?"

Margot stopped taking photos of herself and became fully engaged in the conversation, "You mean to tell us that you *really* have no idea who she is?"

"Other than the most beautiful woman I've ever seen? No. I'm sorry. I can't say that I do."

He was radiating charm, and hearing he had no idea who I

was made everything about him even more intriguing. More enticing. It made him seem more seductive to my lost heart that was just trying to feel again. Trying to *love* again.

From that first encounter, we were never apart. Mitch soon became the one person I had in my life who I could truly be myself around and he never judged me for it.

Around that time, I had just moved into my parents' pool house. I still wanted to be near them, when they were there, but wasn't ready to fully live a life on my own. Bringing Mitch back to my home was where I was able to show him who I really was. I told him about my life and my love of books of all kinds. I told him how no one, besides my parents and Isabelle, whom I kept in contact with, knew this about me. It was my own personal sanctuary I kept locked inside. He made it easy to open up to. He accepted every part of who I was. He loved how much I loved to read and how I knew things about the world most people didn't. He loved how much I loved and admired my parents. And he promised to never tell my friends about the little piece of myself I kept hidden.

He, in return, told me about his modest life growing up in the suburbs of Chicago. He wasn't a real outgoing kid, but always had a fascination with the city and what life in a big city entailed. Which is how he got into "nightlife entertainment" as he called it.

When he was nineteen both of his parents died suddenly, within a few months apart from one another, from pneumonia. After receiving his inheritance, he decided to take the biggest risk of his life and change who he was by reinventing himself. That was something he and I had in common. He started to make investments with the money and before he knew it, he was making millions. That successful endeavor led him into investing into nightclubs. When he helped turn one around in Chicago, another owner asked for his help. He was able to do the same with that establishment, making two competing nightclubs just blocks away from one another. Word began to spread and the next thing he knew, he was being flown to New York and Miami for consulting gigs before taking another leap of faith with investing in himself and his own company.

Now, I don't know much about the financial world, as I've never had anything to do with it before, but when Mitch talked about it, he made me feel like I understood every word he was saying. Describing it in a way that made me feel like I was right there with him. He made life exciting again. He made it something I really looked forward to again since losing the one thing that made me the happiest.

"I will say, you two are a *very* good-looking couple." Franklin leaned in to tell me one afternoon at lunch.

"Thank you!" My heart felt warm, feeling Mitch's acceptance from my friend. "Yeah, he's the most unexpected, *best* thing I could've ever wanted."

"Well, you cleaned him up very well. I see he has an entirely new wardrobe."

"I only had a little to do with that," I smiled. "He was the one who picked everything out. I only picked out a few things I thought brought out the color of his eyes." What they didn't know was that that should've been my first red flag in the life of Mitch Bellamy. Because when he said he had lost his wallet and was waiting for a new credit card to arrive, I volunteered to pay for his shopping spree without batting an eyelash. I was in love and would do anything to make him happy. There was no questioning it.

Mitch was, and still is, in a sense, the most interesting, most hypnotizing man I have ever met. It was no wonder I fell in love with him so fast. Besides Richie, I only knew the love of the characters I fantasized about in books. I had images of a man I loved. So, to have him in real life, almost as if he were straight out of one of my favorite reads, seemed surreal. I think anyone would fall as hard as I did. I mean, doesn't everyone want to be in love? Being in love is such a wonderful feeling. To know someone chooses to care about you deeply and affectionately is remarkable. And you, in return, have those same feelings towards them. Feelings where you can't eat, can't sleep, you just want to be with them every second of the day and even miss them when they're around. It's not right but, everyone else in your life seems to fade away in their importance and you have this uncontrollable urge to shout from mountaintops that you're *in love* with this person. This incredible person who is now number one in your life. You want the entire world to know it. And no matter what people try to tell you, they'll always be wrong about them because you're the *only one* who knows this person and what they're like. You become sacred to one another. You become the only two people in the world who matter.

That was what Mitch Bellamy became to me. He, in a very short period of time, became my, *everything*. I didn't question it because it was what I'd wanted for so long. Someone to love me the way he loved me. What I had been secretly longing for. Someone who adored me. Someone who cherished me. Someone who wanted . . . every part of me.

Chapter Four

"I'm not so sure I trust him, Luke."

"Why Mom? He's perfect. He's Charming. He's smart and successful. Isn't he everything you'd want for your daughter?"

"Those things don't mean anything honey. Those are just words describing him. He hasn't done anything to *prove* himself to us."

"What do you mean? What does he have to prove? He was such a gentleman at dinner last night."

"Anyone can act like a gentleman, Luke. You know that."

She didn't understand. My parents had been together for so long my mother couldn't remember what it was like to fall in love with someone in the beginning. Where everything's new and exciting and feels . . . perfect. You get those rush of feelings where you can't stop smiling when you think of that person. Even though you know you care for them, they make you nervous. You can't help but feel like you're on this never-ending high from being in love. Where every kiss makes you want to keep kissing them. You don't ever want to be apart.

My mother was wrong. She had no idea what she was

talking about. "Mom, you're wrong. Mitch is everything I've ever wanted in a man. Most importantly, he loves me and wants to take care of me. He makes me happy."

"Okay, that's all great, Luke, but who is he *really*? He appeared out of nowhere and there's," she paused. "There's something about him that doesn't settle right with me."

"Like what, mother? He hasn't been anything but lovely to you and dad. Just a gracious, kind man. How can you possibly see anything other than that?"

"When you're a mother you just know these things. You can almost sense them from a mile away. Trust me, Luke, when you're a parent you want nothing but the best for your child and I don't feel like he's it." She took a moment before continuing. "It's in his eyes. They're not kind eyes Luke. They're dark. He doesn't seem like a good person. I can't explain it, honey, but I've taken, and looked at, millions of photographs in my lifetime and you can always tell the good from the bad by looking into someone's eyes. And his are bad. Trust me. He isn't right for you."

"I can't believe this, mom. Are you serious? You're being very judgmental. What happened to looking for the good in people? You have to get to know someone before you can make any assumptions about them because their *eyes* don't look very nice. God, you've barely been there for me my entire life and now all of a sudden you want to play the mom role? You literally met him once, for about two hours. You're ridiculous, you know that, right? You don't know him, and you barely know me. So, how can you even tell me he's not the right one?" I looked at my mother, disappointed she wasn't on my side. "Mitch loves me, and I love him and we're going to be together whether you like it or not."

"You're a grown woman and I can't stop you, Luke. I know that. I just hope you don't come to realize he's a mistake before it's too late and you find yourself, married or pregnant." She sat there looking at me, at the woman I had become. Looking at what I can only describe as feeling *hurt* by my words. "I don't know what else to tell you, honey. I can only give my advice and guidance to you, and you make your mistakes from there."

I knew I had hurt my mother. I lied when I said she hadn't been there for me because she had. She was there, as a mother, in different ways than the typical. But she couldn't put me in a situation where I should base who I was going to love on her knowledge of the depth of someone's eyes. It was absurd.

As if the lack of support from my parents wasn't enough, my friends, who were once supportive of us began asking me weird questions as well.

One evening, at a club, I was in the restroom with Margot who had been acting unlike herself the entire night. Instead of being blunt with me, she seemed kind of adrift, beating around the bush.

When we were reapplying our lipstick, she finally blurted out, "What firm or group did you say Mitch worked with?"

"I don't remember the name. I think he said it was a private equity group he created. Why?"

"Well, I don't want to be rude because I love you and I know he makes you happy, but he gives off a weird vibe. Like *really* weird. So, I asked a few people I know if they knew him, and they'd never heard of him before. They asked if maybe he worked under his holding title?! So, I just wanted to ask. And also, it's weird you don't know the name. I mean . . . ,"

"Well, thanks for the concern, but he's fine. And he doesn't give off a weird vibe, Margot," I scoffed. "You know, you and my mother are starting to sound eerily alike. She said something similar to me the other day." I turned towards her with assertiveness. "Am I missing something? Why do you guys hate the *one* person in my life who makes me the most joyous I've ever been? Like seriously, Margot. What the fuck? What am I not seeing? Because honestly, it feels like all of you are trying to take away someone who makes me feel the best I've ever felt. It's like, I don't know, you're jealous you guys don't have anyone interested in you. It's like we all can't be happy, so you tell me that you fucking hate him."

"We don't hate him. And we're definitely *not* jealous. We're happy for you. We just don't *know* him, and he doesn't really say much to us when we're out together. Like tonight. He's said maybe three words to us. Just simple pleasantries. It's like he doesn't want to get to know how *fabulous* we are."

"I'm sure he's just stressed out with work. I'll talk to him."

"No, don't." She stopped applying her lipstick and threw it in her bag. "That might be a little awkward if he finds out we hate him."

"You just said you didn't, Margot."

"You know what I mean. It could come across that way," she smiled at her reflection before heading out the door and back into the dark, deafening ambience of the club.

I really couldn't see what the problem with Mitch was. He never did or said anything that wasn't absolutely perfect. He came across as a well-educated, well diverse gentleman who had a budding career and who had made something of himself. No one should even question him or his character. So, why were they?

It didn't matter what they thought, though. The decision to love him and be with him was all mine. And I *chose* him. I would *always* choose him. When we were together the world and everything in it felt like it was how it should be. How it was meant to be. It felt spectacular.

"Are you okay? You seem a little down?"

"Oh, yeah, I'm fine. My mom and Margot just said some stuff to me that's been bothering me lately. But I'm okay, I'll get over it."

"What did they say?" He put his arm around my shoulder as he sat down, proving how he was a caring, loving man paying attention to my needs and wanting to be a part of my life.

"I wasn't going to tell you, but I guess I will now," I paused. "They said you give off a bad vibe towards them?! Like, they don't trust you or something. Isn't that ridiculous?" I laughed.

"Of course, it is. And if I'm being honest," he shrugged. "They're so immersed into their lives of being rich and famous, they don't know what it takes to build yourself from the ground up, especially Margot. She's oblivious to the real world because she's had everything handed to her, her entire life. And your Mother," he scoffed. "Well, yes, she built her career as an artist, but so much time in this life has gone to her head. She has *no idea* what it means to be in a world where people aren't doting over her and catering to her every need anymore."

"Well, that isn't entirely true about my mother," I began to say. "Yes, she's used to a certain way of life now, but growing up she was never . . ."

"You're blinded by the fact that she's your mother. I've had enough experience with the nouveau riche since establishing myself amongst them. They've become a fascinating study for me. Trust me."

"But then that would make me . . ."

"No, not you. You're the exception."

"And how's that if I've lived the same way as Margot, having everything handed to me by my mother?"

"Well, you were lucky to have experienced a loneliness that translated to getting lost in literature like most of us in the normal, lower to middle class world. We had television or books to imagine what life would be like in the shoes of another person. Yes, you grew up in that life, but you were lonely and aware of that loneliness which turned your imagination wild with stories of every kind. Luke, you're *astounding*. You could be anything you want to be in this life and with whoever you choose. The possibilities are endless for you." He grabbed my hand, squeezing it gently. "But you're *choosing* to be with me. With a man who came from nothing and still knows what that life is like. You aren't following the paths of your peers or conforming to the pressures of your parents. You're your own person and you know in your heart that you have a beautiful, caring nature who just so happened to be born into a life that only the lonely can dream of," he paused, giving me a little smirk. "You just aren't that person, Luke. You care too deeply for what really matters in life. You care for the human soul. For meaningful relationships. You care for, love. That's why I say you're the exception because you have a pure heart which is rare to find in the only world you know."

He spoke so eloquently, so gentle. He understood me for who I really was. It was comforting to know there was at least one person in this world, in my life, who knew where I came from and what mattered to me most. In that moment, I knew I had fallen in love with Mitch Bellamy. And I knew he was going to be the man I was going to spend the rest of my life with. Everyone was just going to have to get over whatever negative thing they saw in him because Mitch was wonderful. He was more than what I could've ever imagined for myself in a partner. And he was mine.

"I love you, Mitch," I paused in his arms after saying it because I realized we had never said it to one another before. I never wanted to be the first one to say it either because that was what was engrained in my mind since I was a child and could even fathom what the idea of true love was. I started to speak again, "I'm sorry, I . . ."

He put his finger to my lips. "Shh, remember, a beautiful woman should never have to apologize." He kissed me lightly on my forehead and then whispered in my ear, "I love you too."

For the third time in my life, I was in love. This time, it would be different though. This time, it was going to last. He was going to make it last and so was I. Together we were going to make our greatest creation, our life, together.

"I have a wonderful idea," he spouted out in the emotional bliss of the feelings we had just shared.

"What?" I asked, not thinking what he was about to say next was even fathomable.

"We should get married."

I pulled away from his embrace, shocked and elated. "Are you kidding?" I asked questionably.

"No, I would never kid you," he smiled. "I think we should show them how serious we are about each other. What better way to show them all than to get married and really start our life together?"

I sat there feeling an overwhelming mix of emotions. "But we barely know each other. We've only been together for, what, two months? Isn't this a little fast?"

"Not when you're with the right person." He grabbed my hand bringing it up to his heart. "Come on, Luke. I know you feel the same way as I do. You love me. You just said so yourself. Why not *show* me how much you love me by marrying me and continuing to make me the happiest man in the world?"

I couldn't speak. My heart was pounding in my chest and a rush of fear mixed with excitement came over me. As much as I felt like I wanted to say yes, there was a little part of me that wanted to run away. Maybe that was my subconscious warning me. Maybe I should've listened.

"Listen, Luke, I love you and *no one* is going to come in-between that love. I would do *anything* for you. I'd go to the ends of the earth for you and back a *million* times over to prove to you that *you* are the girl for me." He gently put his hand to the side of my face, biting his lower lip into a smile. An innocent act I found irresistible. "Luke, you are my, *everything.* I adore you and I can't imagine my life without you in it. I *need* you in it. You have no idea just how you make me feel. You make me a better person, a better man. You brought me back to life from a point where I was so alone, feeling so lost, not having anyone around. Not even family. But you *are* my family now, Luke. And the *only* person I want to spend my life with. We just have to make it official." He got down on one knee. "What do you say? Will you marry me?"

I knew if I didn't say yes, I would instantly regret it. It was what I wanted, after all. To be happy with a man who loved me. And this man had my entire heart. Who cared if my parents and friends didn't like him? You can't like everybody.

I took a moment to stare into his eyes, to see if I could see the bad my mother was talking about. But all I could see was the blue-gray of the ocean, a place I always loved to visit and get lost in its vastness and beauty. A place that was calming, where I could think and feel like myself when no one else was around. Mitch was my safe place. I hadn't realized until that moment. I was the one who was being ridiculous, letting people get into my head and mess with my feelings.

"Of course, I'll marry you, Mitch! I love you. I love you *so* much." I jumped down into his arms, almost knocking us over to kiss the man who would soon become my husband.

Chapter Five

"No, absolutely not."

I'd never seen my father throw so much assertiveness towards someone in my life. He had always been so caring and understanding with everyone, but for some reason, in that moment with Mitch, he was someone I didn't even recognize.

"Well, with all due respect Orson, Luke is a grown woman and doesn't need your approval to marry me. We were just being cordial and trying to do what she deemed the 'right thing' in asking for your permission."

"I can appreciate that. But I don't like you, Mitch. There's something off about you. I knew it the moment I laid eyes on you," my father began. "I haven't been able to figure it out yet, but I do know, for certain, that I do *not* want you to marry my daughter or be in *my* family in any way whatsoever."

"Dad, that's not fair," I interrupted.

"Luke, I'm telling you, if you marry him, we're cutting you off. I will *not* have someone I *do not* trust in this family."

"Well, it's a good thing I make my own living then."

"Okay. Well, it sounds like you just made your decision.

Good luck." My dad walked away in a way I'd never seen him before. He looked hurt and disheartened, and it was because of me, his daughter, who made him feel that way.

This was the first and only time in my life I had ever defied my parents in any way. Even though deep down it crushed me, I couldn't let anyone see it. I wanted to be with Mitch and if losing my parents, their money and their respect was what was going to happen, then so be it. One day they would come around and see the incredible, smart, brilliant mind of this man I was going to marry. They would be sorry for ever hurting me in the way they were by not accepting the man I loved into their lives.

"I told you they would never give their approval."

"Yeah, I'm sorry I put you through that. I just . . . a part of me was hoping they would be as elated as I am." He was the only person I could be honest with, who made me *feel* like I could be honest back.

"Luke, what do I always tell you?" he snapped.

The abruptness of his question broke me out of the emotions I was lost in. "Umm, what? What- What do you mean?"

"What do I always tell you about apologizing?"

"Oh, uh, that a beautiful woman should never have to apologize."

"Exactly. So, you *definitely* don't need to be apologizing for someone else's negative opinions on us. Those negative ideas are what make them despicable, ugly people and it shows in every word that comes out of their mouths,"

"You're right," I smiled, feeling indifferent to his opinion, yet wanting to please him, but also at the same time, I didn't need to apologize for putting him in a situation where my parents' true colors were showing. I had never even seen that side of them before. Being so unaccepting of someone. It wasn't my problem, and it wasn't my fault.

We eloped the following day in Vegas, of all places. It was not what I had ever envisioned for myself when it came to my wedding. I grew up wanting the fairytale. I wanted the big princess ball gown, the flowers, the 200 plus guest list. I never thought I would be wearing a random white dress I had in my closet from a few summer seasons back. But I made it work. I was happy and in love, so the ensemble didn't matter just as long as the aesthetic and mood for our nuptials was right.

Two hours before departure, Margot, Franklin and Remy reluctantly agreed to attend when I called them to meet us at the airport. I didn't want them to try and talk me out of it, hence the last-minute invitation. But I knew them, and knew they'd never turn down a reason to party. Especially in Vegas where it's a twenty-four-hour party within itself.

Just as we were about to walk down the aisle in the tiny chapel, the doors swung open and in walked my parents.

My face lit up knowing there was no way in the world they would miss the wedding of their only child, whether they approved of it or not.

"Mom! Dad! You came!" My heart filled with joy as I walked over to hug them.

"Luke, we're here to stop you from making the biggest mistake of your life." My mother reached out to grab my hand.

"Orson, Carter, please can . . . "

"Get the fuck away from me," my dad cut him off through gritted teeth, redness rising from his neck up.

"Daddy!"

"Listen, Luke," he turned to face me. "Your mother and I are prepared to do whatever you want or get you whatever you want. A new car, your own house, you name it. Just as long as you don't go through with this and ruin your entire life. We want you to get the fuck away from this man."

"See Luke, just like I told you. They only care about money and not about what's really important in life."

I was in shock, from my father's behavior. It's the complete opposite of what I've always known. My father was tender-hearted and had never said an ill word about anyone. So, to see him like this had me fumbling for my own words to counteract his outburst. Yet, Mitch was right. Why were my parents so frivolous with their bribery? I didn't want any of those things. I could get them myself.

"All I want is for my parents to love and support me on what *should* be the happiest day of my life. Why can't you guys just do that for me?"

"Because you're making a huge mistake, Luke. And I think deep down you know it too sweetheart," my mom pleaded.

"Mom, you of all people should know what it feels like to fall in love with someone who your parents don't approve of. I remember you telling me the story of how your parents didn't like daddy at first, but they came around when they saw what lengths he went through to help get your careers going."

"This is different, honey."

"How? It doesn't seem so different to me."

"Because your grandparents knew dad had a good heart even though he didn't have money," she paused. "Mitch has the money but not a good heart."

"How do you know that? You've never even taken the

time to get to know him. You never even tried. You hated him from the first moment you met him and continued to do so based off of *that* and nothing else."

"Luke, you're still so young and haven't had enough life experience to know the difference between real love and whatever *this* is," my mother gestured towards Mitch.

"You're wrong again. I *do* know what love is because I've experienced it before and never told you. I know what love is supposed to feel like, and what Mitch gives me is *more* love than I've ever felt in real life or have read in any book." I stared at my mother as a tear began rolling down my cheek. The hurt and anger my own parents could place upon me had my heart breaking in a thousand pieces. "You should just go. I don't want you guys here if you aren't going to be happy for me. I don't think I even want to see you ever again." I turned away from my parents and walked up to the man I was spending the rest of my life with. The man who opened my eyes to a world I didn't even know existed. A world that wasn't surrounded by what some would call the "finer things." It was surrounded by things that were grounded, which was something I don't think I had ever truly been around before. Mitch made me realize that there was more to life, more to me.

My parents left the chapel, without turning back, and I walked down the aisle where I became Mrs. Mitch Bellamy. I was the happiest woman in the world. It was now time to start living in a way I had only ever read about. But first, it was time to celebrate.

~

"I can't believe you actually married him," Remy yelled into my ear over the loud music.

"Why?" I yelled back.

"It's just so unlike you to make such an uncalculated move."

"Well, sometimes the uncalculated moves are the ones worth taking."

"But is he the one worth taking it for?"

"Please don't tell me that *you're* going to give me crap about him too, Remy. That's the *last* thing I need. And besides, he's my husband now, so it doesn't matter anyway."

"I won't, I promise. But if you ever need me, don't hesitate to call and I'll come get you in a heartbeat." He looked at me with such sincerity in his eyes, I could actually feel the depth of his words and the concern behind them. Remy wasn't so sure about him either.

It was frightening to be hit with the thought that maybe I *had* made a mistake. But although I had that feeling, I still couldn't see what was wrong with Mitch. What was I missing? I didn't understand why they couldn't see what I saw in him, what I saw in my sweet, charming man. All I could think of was that they didn't know him privately. They didn't know the Mitch I knew when we were alone together. The Mitch who listened to every word I said and paid attention to every detail because he wanted to feel like he had been a part of my whole life. He wanted to make me feel like I could trust him because it would make me feel safe. And it did. I did.

When he was with my friends, he was never aggressive or demanding in any way. He was mostly silent and only spoke when they asked him questions. So, he didn't give away much information about his personal life. That was none of their business. It was only mine to know, when he shared it, and mine only. If I had the choice to live a private life, I would, it just wasn't the hand my life was dealt.

We said our goodbyes to my three friends and went to Miami for a brief little honeymoon. Mitch said he had to check out a property but would make it worth my while if I agreed to go with him. I was now his wife. I wanted to make him happy and honestly, I didn't care where we went on our honeymoon. I didn't care if we even went on one at all. I just wanted to be with my husband.

I was so in love with Mitch that nothing would ever make me think of him any different. He was, and had always been, the same man who impressed me from just a little stare. He was the smart, impressive man who made me fall in love with him the instant I first saw him. I don't know how else to explain what I felt for him other than saying he was the absolute love of my life. I had loved before, but not in the way I loved Mitch. I knew he was going to do great things and I was happy to be by his side supporting him along the way. He, in return, was by my side, bringing me back to life from the heartache I had hidden so deep down inside of me. He was, like I had said, the third love of my life. And what is it that they say about the third? Third times the charm? Well, he was that and then some. Until he wasn't . . .

Chapter Six

I want to state now, that this next part was reiterated to me later, as I was not there when this conversation was taking place. It's a very important part of my story because it shows the lengths the people I love went through to try and help me, which I will forever be grateful to them for.

While Mitch and I were in Miami on our honeymoon, Remy called my mother and asked her to meet him, Margot and Franklin for lunch. My mother agreed and this is what happened:

"Hello, Mrs. Townsend."

"Please, call me Carter. We've known each other far too long now." They proceeded to kiss each other's cheeks and sat down. "So, this is a little unexpected. We've never done this before."

"Well," Franklin began. "We're a little concerned about Luke."

"You can sense it too?" My mother asked.

"Yes," Margot said. "We don't trust him. And it's not like we would usually pry into someone's life or disrupt whatever they had going on, but we've just never really cared for him. He's always been a bit creepy. I'm sure you know what I mean."

"The staring," My mother uttered.

"And that look of almost," Franklin paused in his thought for the right word to say. "Evil."

"Not to mention he'd been following her around, staring at her even though he said it was for work," Remy added.

"We've even joked he was a stalker," Margot stated.

"But umm," Remy hesitated. "She's just changed so much since meeting him. It's like he controls her," he paused. "And Margot even asked some people she knows about him, but no one seems to know who he is," he paused again, looking to Margot and Franklin before landing on my mother. "We're worried about her."

"Her father and I are worried too," my mother began. "We've actually been in touch with a private investigator to see if they can find out who this guy really is. We've never gotten a good feeling from him and when we've looked online, we can't find anything about a Mitch Bellamy in private equity or having anything to do with nightclubs. There aren't any pictures either that even remotely resemble him. It's a bit scary to think that Luke is with someone she really doesn't even know or even exists."

They said my mother looked frightened, like they could see how much pain and worry she was in although she was trying to mask it by keeping it together. She was just being a good mother, trying to save her daughter from someone she knew in her gut, was a bad person. A *very* bad person. But to me, he was still just Mitch. My perfect, *loving* husband.

"What can we do to help?" Margot urged. "We need to get her away from this guy. He's such a creep."

"Yes, Carter, what can we do?" Remy grabbed my mother's hand and held it tightly in his.

"You three are such great friends. She's lucky to have you," my mother smiled. "I don't know if she ever told you this but, she didn't have any real friends growing up. We kind of always toted her around with us even though we had said we wanted her to have a normal life. That was our fault. We didn't uphold our end of what we wanted for her. So, you would always just see her at our gallery parties with her nose in a book."

"Luke?" Franklin questioned.

"Yes, she's very well versed in literature, more so than a lot of the scholars I know. She's a lot smarter than she leads on which is why she can probably play the airhead, socialite persona she does so well. She's quite brilliant actually. To think of it, I don't think I've ever told her that."

"That makes a lot of sense," Remy said. "I knew there was a reason why she's always so calculated with everything. She's always so many steps ahead of us."

"Well, it's just a shame she isn't with this one," my mother sighed. "For someone so smart who's been around as many people as she has, you'd think she could read them like a book. But I guess what they say about love being blind is proving to be true in the situation we are finding ourselves in now. He has her under some kind of spell she can't see her way past."

"Hopefully we can get her to see what we're all seeing and snap her out of it," Margot said. "I mean, even if she's in love with him, how does she not see how cringy he is?" She shuddered. "And also, I mean I get how he could get into the clubs, but how in the hell did he get into the Polo match? I keep wondering that. Like, who let him in?"

"I keep thinking about that god awful wedding and what she said to us when we were trying to stop her. You know about her experiencing love before. We've never known her to have been in a relationship before. She never . . ."

"She was talking about Richie," Remy interrupted, looking down.

"Who?"

"He was her first love. They met when we were nineteen. They were the cutest, actually," he smiled.

"We *loved* him," Margot emphasized.

"She never mentioned him," my mother said, somberly.

"Yeah, well, they were really in love. He made Luke light up like I've never seen before. They were wonderful for each other and complimented one another perfectly. He's a musician so he was so fun to be around. He brought out a different side of Luke, a playful side. When we met him, they instantly fell for each other," Franklin said.

"Why wouldn't she tell us about him?"

"You and Mr. Townsend were spending more time than usual in New York that year. I think you were having a huge opening and Luke kind of found this person who was there for her and she kind of clung to him. But in a good way. Richie was really good for her. I mean, we all thought they were going to get married," Remy smirked.

"And they almost did," Margot butted in.

"What?" My mother sat there in shock as she was just finding out about such an important part of my life that she had no idea ever happened.

"Well, I don't know how to say this without being blunt, so," Remy let out a breath. "They got pregnant a few months in, and Richie proposed to Luke." My mother's eyes widened in disbelief. "They were planning on getting married and moving somewhere where they could start a normal life together. But—" Remy paused, looking at Franklin and Margot's saddened faces. "The baby passed when Luke was five months pregnant, and it absolutely *crushed* her. It crushed both of them."

"Why wouldn't she tell me any of this? I should have been there for her." My mother started to tear up. "She must've been in such heartache." My friends said they could see the pain in her eyes.

Remy continued, "Well, Richie ended up cheating on her after they lost the baby and left her which," he gestured with his hands, "Didn't help how sad she already was for losing the baby. But we were there and tried to help her through it as best as we could, not ever experiencing anything like that ourselves. Then one day, Luke just, became a new person."

"Yeah, she became the Luke the world knows now. Or, knew before Mitch," Franklin said. "She kind of just pushed everything down as if it didn't even happen. It was strange at first to see, but we're talking about Luke, and nothing really surprises me with her until now."

"Thank you for telling me all of this," my mother said. "And thank you for taking care of her. You three are more than she could ever deserve, and you have my complete and utter gratitude." My mother took a moment to collect herself. "Well, I should've been there, but I can't think of that right now. I have to think about helping her and being there for her in *this* moment when she needs me the most. I think we should keep in contact with one another and *please* let us know if you see or hear anything else suspicious about that asshole and how he's treating her. We need to get him away from her. From all of us."

"I think that's a good idea," Remy agreed. "I've tried to

text her a few times, but she isn't responding as quickly as she usually does. Even at that, her texts seem so unlike her. I guess I can justify it by saying they're on their honeymoon . . ." my mother scoffed, "But it's just, weird and not like her."

"I agree. I tried calling her and she was so short with me," Margot said. "I just wanted to say hi and see how things were going, and she just said she had to go because they were going to the pool and she couldn't talk. You would think she could give at least *five* minutes to one of her best friends. But I could hear him in the background trying to get her to leave."

"I'm just so nervous something bad is going to happen," my mother said. "I have such a terrible feeling."

"Remy, its Carter and Orson. We're on speaker phone."

"Hi Carter, hello Orson. Is everything okay? I haven't heard from Luke in a few days."

"We've just received a text letting us know they'll be home later tonight. But I wanted to tell you, our private investigator got back to us, and we know who he is."

"Mitch?"

"Yes, Remy. And you're not going to believe it . . ."

"Well, tell me. Is he . . ."

"His name isn't Mitch Bellamy that's for sure, it's Jason Feldstein."

"What?"

"Yes, and he's from Yellow Springs, Ohio. Where he's been arrested for petty crimes and was even charged, but never convicted for two murders."

"Carter. No!" Remy said, breathless.

"Yes. We *have* to get her out of this but we have to do it

strategically, so she won't resist us. We can't have anything bad happen to her or any of us along the way," my father said.

"I agree. Do you have any ideas?"

"We have a call with our lawyer and a strategist this afternoon to inform them of the situation and to get whatever help we can as he really isn't doing anything other than using a fake name. It's all just basic information right now. We are waiting to hear more, but just the fact that he is using a fake name makes us feel like we need to figure out what he plans to do with Luke and why he chose her."

"I'm so terrified," my mom began to cry.

"It's okay, honey, we're going to get this bastard away from her."

"Oh my god. I can't believe this is happening. We *all knew* there was something shady about him. I just can't believe Luke could fall for all of his bullshit. For his bullshit façade. I can't even think of a reason why he would choose *her* of all people. Why her? Why Luke? And just that word, him *choosing* her. Do you really think that's what he did?"

"That's what we're going to find out," my dad said. "I can't believe we let this happen. That we let it get this far. It's my fault. I'm her father. How could I've let this happen?"

"It isn't your fault Orson. You couldn't have known. None of us could've. He literally appeared into our lives and now we're *here*. But we're going to figure it out. We have to! You guys have all the resources and Margot, Franklin and myself, are here to help in any way we can. If you need us to be ploys, kidnap her, whatever it takes. We're willing to do whatever. I just . . . can't imagine what you guys are going through. I'm so sorry."

"Thank you, Remy. That means a lot," my mother said to him. "There's just a small glimmer of hope in this, which is knowing we're going to have a plan soon. God, I just . . ."

She broke down in loud cries. "I'm shaking. I can't get rid of this pit in my stomach that something bad is going to happen if it hasn't already."

"Well, it's not good to think that way. That'll only make it worse," Remy consoled her.

"I know. Thank you, sweetie," she paused. "We'll keep you updated on what we come up with and if, like you said, we could use you to help out. We really appreciate it."

Chapter Seven

Later that night Mitch and I arrived home. The car dropped us off in the front of the property so we had to walk around back to get to the pool house. I was a little surprised my parents hadn't kicked us out yet or had the locks changed. But knowing what I know now, it was probably because they wanted to keep me close by, to protect me. That makes my heart happy knowing they were doing whatever they could to help me get out of what was to come.

My parents must've heard the car pull up because as we were walking to the pool house they came out onto the back patio.

"Hi, Luke," my mom yelled.

"What? No hi to their son-in-law?" Mitch mocked.

I was about to say hello back when Mitch grabbed the arm I was going to wave with. I caught the look on my mother's face and instantly snapped, "What are you doing?"

"Don't give her the satisfaction. She's not worth it."

"But she's still my mom."

"Luke, she cut you off because she didn't want you to marry me. That's a narcissist if I ever saw one. We don't need that toxicity in our life. Come on, keep going." He nudged me in the back of my right shoulder causing me to stumble a few steps.

"Luke," my mother called, "Luke, we're here if you need us. Just call out and we'll come running. Please be careful honey, please! I love you," she paused. "And Jason if you so much as hurt one hair on her head I'll kill you myself."

Mitch froze. I didn't catch it. I think I was still in shock of how he had grabbed my arm. He pushed me inside of the pool house and locked the door immediately. Then he began to tell me how we had to figure out where we wanted to live because he couldn't live on the same property as two people who were so disgusting as to hate him for marrying their daughter. That's where the night ended. Just the two of us. In our own little world. In love.

Chapter Eight

s I lied in his arms after making love, I listened to the slow rhythms of his heartbeat feeling as though I were in a state of bliss. He was my husband and I loved him, but there was a lingering thought in the back of my mind that wouldn't allow me to succumb to the complete feeling of satisfaction. There was something different. Making love to him felt different. It didn't seem as intimate, or passionate as it had before. It suddenly felt cold, hard and rushed. I wouldn't really even call it making love. It felt more like he was just trying to get a quick one in. A simple fuck.

I tried brushing the thought off, thinking we just had an off night, but when I heard his heart begin to beat faster, the feeling of dissatisfaction turned to concern.

"Are you okay? You seem a little anxious right now."

"I'm never anxious. Being anxious is for the weak."

"Okay " I looked away, brow raised, wondering where his outburst had come from.

"We need to leave this property." He adjusted to look at me. "What would you say if we moved to Connecticut or Massachusetts?"

"Why not New York?" I suggested. "That way we could still be close to everyone."

"I don't want to be close to anyone, I only want to be close to you. And besides, those two places are close enough to New York. One by train, one by plane. We could make day trips if we needed."

"But what about the club you're planning on opening here in L.A.? Won't that be a little much having to fly back and forth all the time?"

"Yeah, I've been thinking about that. I'm going to scrap that project. I talked to my business partner already and he agreed it doesn't make sense right now."

"Business partner?" I questioned. "I didn't know you had one. I thought you did everything by yourself?"

"No, I have a business partner."

"You've just never mentioned them bef—"

"I don't need to tell you everything," he said, shortly. "I'm sure I've talked about him before. I know I have."

I had my own anxious feelings arise as Mitch completely caught me off guard. One, he'd never mentioned a business partner before. And two, I was now his wife. He should be telling me everything. At least that's what I thought married couples did.

"Oh yeah, maybe I just forgot." I shied away like the woman in love that I was, ignoring it and dropping the subject to appease my new husband. I wanted to make him happy. I didn't want to be one of those celebrities who had a quickie marriage. I wanted this to last.

I couldn't sleep much that night. There was something else

lingering in the back of my mind which I couldn't quite put my finger on.

As I lied there recounting the events of the evening, I soon landed on what I thought was the culprit of my unsettling thoughts. Mitch had never hurt me in any way before. So, when he grabbed my arm and nudged me, I didn't think of it as being anything other than him being annoyed by my mother. But every time I tried to close my eyes, I couldn't help but see the look on her face. Her eyes bulging, hands clasped to her chest wanting to run and save me, but seemingly frozen in place. I started to question why she didn't run over. I would have if I saw someone treating my daughter the way Mitch was treating me then.

I shook off the thought, telling myself he loved me, but then another question began to swirl around my mind. What was it exactly everyone was so worried about, besides one little moment of misjudgment on his part? That was the first time he'd ever done anything like that to me and of course it had to be the *one time* someone was watching. Not that it would be any different in private, but it only could lead to untrue assumptions about him. About us.

Sleep wouldn't come. I continued to lie there listening to the sound of his heavy breathing and light snoring when that nagging thought in the back of my mind finally clicked.

My mother called him something other than Mitch. But the name was lost to me. I just knew it was different. That had to have been a mistake on her part. She was a sharp woman. She was just scared to see her daughter being handled in an unpleasant manner.

I replayed what happened over and over trying to remember what she had called him, but every time, it kept playing back as a muffled sound. Almost like I didn't want to know.

When morning arrived, and Mitch woke up, I let him ease into his normal routine with the intent of asking him what my mother had called him the evening before. I wanted to ask if there was something he wasn't telling me because it started to feel like there was. Like I was out of the loop on something important everyone knew but me. But with how odd his behavior was starting to become, I felt like I had to be careful. I didn't want to make him mad. Or see what he would look like, or do, if he were.

After we ate breakfast, Mitch sat on the couch where he started to look at real estate on my laptop. The anxiety was eating me alive as I watched him from the kitchen. I couldn't hold it in. So, I finally blurted it out, "Hey Mitch? Umm . . ." But the words could barely form. "When we got home yesterday and had that interaction with my mother, I could've *sworn* she called you something other than Mitch. Was she mistaken? Or am I?"

He slowly raised his head. His eyes in a dead glare, revealing a man hiding a secret behind them. "I didn't hear her call me by another name. But if she did, it was her fault. She's probably senile which doesn't surprise me. That's probably why she's so neurotic about her not wanting us to be together."

"Oh, okay. That makes sense. I just could've sworn she . . ."

"Luke, how many times am I going to have to tell you to forget about them? They don't want to be happy for us. So, why do you continue to give them the benefit of the doubt? You need to block them from your life. From *our* life."

I wanted to do what he said because he was my husband and I was a loving, obeying wife. But there was a part of me, the Luke *Fucking* Townsend part who wanted to resist him and these specific ill wishes towards my parents. I mean, they were *my parents*. My *blood*. The ones who gave me life. They loved me more than *anyone* ever *would* or *could*. I only knew that because I experienced it myself even though it was for such a short time. As a respectful, loving wife, I agreed with him because that's what I thought marriages were about, siding with one another even when you know the other person is wrong. When I married Mitch, I left Luke *Fucking* Townsend behind and became Mitch's other half. Together we were one. It was an unintentional reinvention of myself coming from a place that as you know from hearing my story, was buried deep down inside of me.

What was even more unintentional than that, was losing a part of myself and being hidden by a man I thought I owed my life to.

"I think you should go out with your friends tonight."

"What? Really?" I was shocked by his suggestion. "Are you going to come?" I asked, feeling happy he was *allowing* me to see my friends after him telling me I should leave them behind as well. It kind of confused me, but I didn't think anything of it because I was too excited he was *letting* me see them.

"No, I think it's important for you to see them alone." He sounded so matter of fact. "I don't always need to be there. You guys can talk about makeup or shoes or whatever it is you talk about."

"Mitch," I looked to him in defense of my friends. "We aren't that pathetic."

"Could've fooled me," he scoffed. "I've been ear shot to a lot of your conversations and they seem pretty mindless to me." He paused, looking up at me as I had now joined him on the couch. "But go and have some fun. Just don't drink too much. I don't like it when you drink."

"I promise, I won't. I usually never do. I've just been so

happy lately. I've kind of let my guard down a few times to really feel every bit of this happiness."

"And who gives you that happiness?" He nodded towards me in a sexy dominating kind of way.

"You." I smiled, taking my laptop from his lap and climbing up onto him, straddling my husband. "You, Mitch. *You* give me that happiness." I smiled as I inched towards his face, my breath falling heavy as I lingered near his lips. Then I whispered, "You make me the happiest woman in the world." We teased one another with our mouths. Our tongues grazing slightly over each other's before I whispered again, "I love you so much." Then we fell into a hard, all consuming, passionate kiss.

After quickly unzipping his jeans, he grabbed the sides of my thighs, firmly pulling me closer to him. Once he was inside me, he was rough like he'd been the night before. It was as if he'd lost the gentle, passionate love making side of him which was one of the things that made me fall even more in love with this already perfect man. It was the side of him that made me want more. It was the part that made me want to defend him to everyone. He was now just there, with nega-tive, empty thrusts that didn't convey any type of affection or love for me, his wife. I grimaced a couple of times from the force he was exerting. When I let out a whimper of pain he grabbed my hair, pulling my head back roughly. "You feel that power? That's your fucking husband right there."

I didn't want to keep going. I wanted to push him off of me. I wanted to get away from him. I never wanted a man to treat me like that. But now someone who'd never been anything but loving towards me was treating me like a piece of meat. It seemed as if he were getting a kick out of what was happening. Like he had control over me and enjoyed it. Then that new part of me, who only wanted to please my husband, told me to not upset him because I didn't want him to take back letting me be able to see my friends. So, I let him finish.

After, when I went to take a shower, I texted Margot, Franklin and Remy to meet me at The Polo Lounge for dinner.

During my shower, I couldn't shake the looming feeling hanging over me. No matter how hard I tried, I couldn't get the water hot enough. I felt like I needed to wash away what had just happened. But I also didn't really know *what* had just happened. Mitch seemed different in a way I couldn't quite explain.

Once we sat down after saying our hellos, Remy immediately started in on me. "Luke, where have you been? We've all tried calling and texting but it's like you're ignoring us."

"Well, we only got back from Miami last night and I haven't been on my phone much. Mitch likes to have uninterrupted conversations and says phones are such distractions these days. And I agree. My mind is so much clearer since I've been staying off of it."

"You? Not on your phone?" Margot cocked her head as if she was never the one always on hers.

"Well, I was never on it as much as *you* are Margot."

"Even still," she straightened up trying to exude dominance over me. "I find it hard to believe you would just . . . give it up. That's strange."

"Not really," I replied. "Sometimes when you meet someone and fall in love, they teach you things you would never normally realize on your own." I paused. "And in this case, it's the damaging effects of being on my phone all of the time. That constant need for myself to be thrust into the spotlight. It's worn me down a bit."

"What's his IG?"

"He doesn't have one."

"What about Facebook? TikTok? Whatever?!"

"He doesn't have them."

"Okay, red flag number one," Margot scoffed. "Luke, you can't trust a person who doesn't have socials. Come on, not even a finsta?"

"No. He likes his privacy and I respect that."

"What about for his business? He *has* to have something for that."

"No, he said he likes to stay behind the scenes. Word of mouth is what gets him new clients. Apparently, in that whole world, that's how it works."

"How do you know?"

"He told me."

"And you believe him?"

"Of course I do. I trust him."

Margot rolled her eyes. "You can trust someone and still not believe them."

They knew the subject needed to be changed.

"Okay, well, other than all that, how've you been? How's married life?" Franklin smiled, seeming genuinely curious.

"It's great! I highly recommend it," I smirked, hoping my remark got to Margot. "You know, I never thought I'd ever find someone I would love more than I loved Richie. I mean, you know how special he was to me. But then Mitch came along, and it's just been incredible to feel that feeling again."

"What feeling is that exactly?" Remy questioned.

"You know, those feelings you only feel in the beginning when you're just starting to fall in love with someone. I didn't think I'd ever feel them again. I'm just . . . lucky enough to be experiencing them for the second time. I don't think many people get that."

Margot rolled her eyes again.

"I know you hate him Margot but you're my friend. You can at least *pretend* to be happy for us. For *me*."

"I don't play pretend Luke. I know I'm a bitch and I fully live up to what people perceive me to be. So, if I want to roll my eyes at a fucking dumb comment, I will."

"Ladies, please!" Remy took control of our bickering. "Let's just make this dinner about the four if us being together again and put all the cattiness aside while we have Luke here with us for once *without* her better half."

"Better?" Margot scoffed.

I glared at her about ready to throw my champagne in her face. An act very out of character for myself.

"Her *other* half," Remy corrected himself.

"I second that," Franklin acknowledged his agreeance by raising his glance.

"Okay, fine," I agreed.

"Sure, whatever," Margot shrugged, before looking down at her phone.

"Great! So," Franklin began. "How was Miami? Did you miss us?"

"It was fun! Umm," I paused. "You know it was a little weird actually."

"How so?" Remy asked.

"Well, I thought we were going to look at a potential nightclub property out there because that's what Mitch had said," I put my focus onto Remy. "But we literally just stayed at the hotel the entire time. I mean, he did go to a meeting or two, but was never gone for very long. I honestly don't even think he left the property."

"That is weird," Franklin narrowed his eyes.

"Well, how was it getting home last night? Did you see your parents? Or talk to them?" Remy asked, seeming a bit eager about the interaction.

"I saw my mom for about two seconds," I answered. "They were on the patio, and we were closer to the pool house. She yelled hi over to me and told me that if I needed her to not hesitate to call." I shook off my answer, then smiled at my friends happy to be with them.

"Well, that's good. She's showing she really cares for you," Remy grabbed my hand and gave it a squeeze.

"Yeah. Maybe she's more open to you and Mitch being together now that you two are *actually* married." Franklin widened his eyes, trying to seem positive. Knowing what I know now, his look takes on a different meaning.

"But then something really weird happened and I couldn't sleep all night thinking about it."

"What happened?" Margot piped up, seeming interested in what could possibly be some gossip.

"She, ummm . . . called Mitch by another name." I paused, thinking about it. "I can't remember what it was, but he started acting a little off after that, saying we needed to move away as soon as possible." The three of them exchanged knowing glances. "What? Why are you looking at each other like that?"

"Nothing. That *is* really weird," Remy said. "Maybe she was just thinking of something else, and a different name came out," he suggested.

"Yeah, it happens to me *all* the time," Margot admitted.

"I don't know. I'm not going to let myself lose anymore sleep over it. I'm just so excited to be here with you guys right now. When Mitch suggested it, I . . ."

"Wait, he told you to come out with us?" Margot interrupted.

"Yeah, he said I should hang out with my friends. So, here we are!" I gestured to them. "Is that weird to you?"

"No. I'm just a little surprised he didn't want to be glued to your arm."

"Margot, I really hope that one day you find someone you're in love with just so you can see *exactly* how it feels to love someone *so much,* that you only want to be around them. You only want to talk to them, or see them every day. And that they make you so *unbelievably* happy that nothing else matters anymore. It's a really great feeling, Margot, you should try it sometime. Until then, shut the fuck up."

"Fine, jeez. You don't have to be such a bitch." She rolled her eyes. "We get it. You're in love."

I turned my attention to the two who actually cared about me. "Well, I think we should make a toast," I raised my glass. "To us! To our futures! And to wishing each other nothing but happiness!" I glanced at Margot, forcing her to unwillingly smile.

"To us!" Remy raised his glass.

"To us!" I said, meeting his glass with mine.

We had a few drinks during dinner. We were celebrating. To be exact, I only had two. Not too much as to where I was drunk, but enough to feel a little buzzed. I was still in control at a level where Mitch wouldn't have been able to detect I'd even been drinking.

When I got home, I parked my car and began my walk to the pool house when something strange caught my eye. All of the drapes to my parents' home were drawn. They never drew the drapes because my mother loved to look out and admire the landscape. She said it gave her inspiration no matter what time of day. I thought it was a little bit funny, but I kept walking to my door where I found a note taped to it.

Meet me in the main house. I love you.
-M.

I turned towards the house filled with excitement thinking that maybe me going out with my friends was some sort of distraction. That my parents had miraculously reconciled with Mitch and were throwing us a surprise party to celebrate our wedding.

I don't know why I felt the need to knock. The smile on my face was met with no answer. The excitement started to well up inside me, picturing everyone jumping out to yell, "SURPRISE!" when I opened the door. I imagined every person I cared about smiling and happy.

I took a deep breath and began to turn the handle, "Hello?" I called, softly. "Mitch? Mom? Dad? Are you guys here?" The door was fully open as I began to walk into the dimly lit room. "You guys can come out now. I know what you're up to," I laughed. "You know I hate surprises. Come on! Where are you?" There was still no answer.

I could see a faint light in the distance, past the foyer, in the formal living room. So, I began to make my way there. "What is this? Why aren't you guys answering me?" My excitement started to fade, and an uneasiness began to grow.

I took the last step through the entry way of the room, and I froze.

I saw them.

My parents.

And as my eyes grew with shock, I was met with darkness.

Chapter Nine

My eyes shot open. A gasp of air filling my lungs as panic washed over me not knowing what had happened or where I was. Breathing heavily, the familiarity of the room started to make sense in my mind as I began to feel more conscious. I blinked, shaking my head a few times trying to steady the rapidity of my breathing, but was met with the terrible image I knew I could never un-see.

My parents, my beautiful parents, were tied up directly in front of me. Their mouths covered with tape. Their eyes filled with terror and worry.

The panic I had thought was subsiding, returned again, quickly causing my heart to race. Immediately, I tried to get up to rush over to help them. But the realization of not being able to move tore through me as I found myself in the same position they were in. Trapped. Tied to a chair.

With fear and trepidation presented before me, I started to scream "Help! Help! Mitch! Where are you? Help us! What the fuck is this?" I cried. "Untie us right now!"

As if on cue, right out of a horror movie, he entered the room, slowly, withdrawn from his surroundings. A dead expression filled his face. His eyes, pinching together, in the way only a villain would.

He was glaring at the one person who loved him. *Me*. But this was *not* the man I had fallen in love with. He was a lost and tortured soul out to get revenge on the one person he loved and the two she loved.

I couldn't help but be scared because the one man whom I loved and trusted, had me in a position any woman would never want to find herself in. With no way to defend myself and scared out of my mind not knowing what could happen next. Someone who loves you doesn't put fear in your life. Especially in your heart.

"What the fuck are you doing? Untie me now!" I yelled again.

With the slightest tilt of his head and the unfamiliar, sinister look of evil, he uttered, "Now why would I do that?"

The coldness of his words ran through me. "Mitch," I quivered, tears teetering the edge of my lower lids. "This isn't funny, let us go. Please."

He took a step back and faced my parents. "I'm doing what needs to be done, Luke."

In that instant, I knew I had done it. I had made the mistake my dad kept saying I was making. I didn't listen. I was too stubborn and too in my own head to see through this man who had bullshitted his way into my life, into making me fall in love with him. None of that mattered anymore, though, because I was now there, letdown, and not only by him, but mostly by myself.

The man before me was a stranger. Leaving me to feel hopeless, heartbroken and scared. His eyes were now dark. Empty. The Mitch I knew was nowhere to be seen. Nowhere to even reach. He had vanished.

My breathing began to quicken as the tears were slowly

rolling down my cheeks in rapid streams. The only clear thought that came to mind was how I knew I had to be strong to save my parents. To save myself. I would be the only one who could do it.

So, as I calmed myself, I managed to get out, "What are you talking about?" in a means to evade what I was hoping wouldn't come.

"You know they're never going to be okay with us."

"Mitch, please," my voice quaked. "Untie me and we can go about this in a different way."

"No, Luke, I won't," he snapped. "You know, I was wrong about you. Or, well, I think I always knew. I just started to believe the lies I was telling you."

"What are you talking about?"

"You're just like her."

"Like who?"

"Your bitch mother."

"Don't call her that."

"But it's true."

"Mitch. Let. Me. Go," I demanded.

"Yeah, just like her, only thinking about herself," he began. "I knew when she called me Jason," he smirked. "That clever, sneaky little bitch was up to something. So, I . . ."

"She *did* call you by another name," I interrupted. I knew it. "Who are you?" I yelled. "And why in the hell are you doing this to us, Jason? Unti . . ."

"MY FUCKING NAME IS MITCH!" he screamed. "Come on, you know this, Luke," he continued, calmly. "You know me. I'm your husband. The one who fucks you and makes you happy. I'm the one you love and the only one you trust." He slowly started to walk towards me. "My name is Mitch Bellamy, YOUR FUCKING HUSBAND," he yelled again. "And I'm getting *really* tired of being interrupted when

I'm trying to explain this to you." He grabbed a roll of duct tape sitting nearby and ripped a piece off.

Knowing what he was about to do, I wet my lips as much as I could and began wiggling around hoping it would make it harder for him to cover my mouth properly, but that only got him more upset.

He put his hands around my neck and began to squeeze, shaking my head vigorously. "STOP FUCKING MOVING."

I knew I had to listen to him because if I didn't, I might not come out of it alive, and neither would my parents.

I forced myself to relax and resisted the urge to fight back. It was the hardest thing to do when all I wanted was to just save us. Save *them*.

"There, good girl." He took a step back, admiring his work. "Now where was I? Oh yes! Your clever, bitch of a mother. I knew she was up to something when she called me Jason." He walked over to her, but not before grabbing a large butcher's knife from the table beside me. "So, now Carter, my only question is *why* would you call me Jason when you clearly know my name is Mitch? Did someone get a little nosy and have someone else look into me? Because I know you couldn't do it yourself." He grazed the blade against my mother's throat.

The look of sheer terror my mother gave me will be a look I won't ever forget, knowing it was all because of me.

"Or was it you, Orson?" He flicked the knife before my father, draining the color from his face.

The man I had only ever known as strong, fearless, a stoic, turned into a scared, helpless man knowing he wouldn't be able to protect his family right before my eyes.

"I know *you* hate me the most. No one could ever be good enough for your precious little Luke. But guess what?" He bent over to whisper in my father's ear. "Guess who she calls daddy when I'm fucking her all night?"

My father closed his eyes, but I could see the pain he was trying to conceal pour out of him. I knew I had let my father down. All I felt was shame and embarrassment because how would he ever trust me or even look at me the same way again?

Then the cries I was holding in began to rush out of me, knowing that the only reason this was happening to him, to them, was because of me. Because I was so *stupid* in letting this man into my life.

Mitch had taken everything away from me. I couldn't think or see my way out of this. That couldn't be it though. That couldn't be how everything was going to end. We would get through it because there was no way for us not to. I remember starting to feel hopeless because there wasn't anything I could do.

But I couldn't care about myself, there was no time to with everything taking place before me. I wasn't important. And although I felt helpless by not being able to get up and help them or even use my words to get us out of this, I needed to try, or at least feel like I was trying.

Mitch began to pace back and forth, making a nonsensical rant about how life wasn't fair. "Society puts us down. They make us think we can have it all, but the only way that shit can happen is if you go out and take it for yourself. That's what I'm doing," he said. "I'm taking it for myself."

Mitch, Jason, left the room for a brief moment before returning with another large knife. "I think this one might be a little sharper." He held the knife up, examining the blade. "You know how I like things neat and tidy," he winked.

"Did I ever tell you about my childhood, Luke?" His crazed look turned to a smile. "I don't think I did," he paused

"Well, I grew up in a *very* small town where everybody knew everybody. Now as idyllic as that sounds, it's only like that if you come from a good family. Not when you're the kid of the town whore and the town drunk. Growing up people made fun of me for that." He looked at me, expressionless. "I was the town bastard." He kept his gaze on me for a moment longer before continuing. "And for fucks sakes, kids can be so fucking cruel." He raised his arm above his head, bringing it down with the force of the knife to a pillow. "No one ever understood me. They never knew I was actually smart. They assumed I was just like my parents. Dumb as shit." He raised the knife once more, thrashing it down into the pillow. "At a young age I understood that, and I let them think it. So, yes, I did eventually fall into some trouble, but it was only because people expected it from me. Give them what they want. Am I right, Luke?"

I sat there staring at him, trying to convince him with my eyes that he didn't need to do this; that everything would be okay if he would just let us go. I was trying to tell him that we wouldn't turn him in. We would forget all about it, but it's hard to make someone read your mind, when they don't want to read it.

"Oh, don't look at me like that," he snapped. "This is happening, but don't worry because you're my wife. *You'll* be fine."

My eyes widened, the intensity of the situation beginning to set in. I was coming to the realization that if I *did* make it out alive, my parents were most likely *not*. I tried to scream and yell. I tried to make any noise I could to get someone's attention who wasn't there. It only made him more upset.

He ran to me, holding the knife against my throat. "Do you want me to kill you too?" I shook my head no. "Then you better fucking shut up and obey your husband."

My breathing shook as I nodded my head in agreement.

He walked back over to my parents and continued his rant. "I knew right after I murdered those two girls and got away with it, I needed to turn my life around. I needed a fresh start. I needed a change." My heart sank. I was stunned. He had murdered before?! "So, one day when I was at the grocery store, I just so happened to walk down the aisle with magazines, and you know what I saw?" He looked at me with a devilish look on his face. "The most beautiful woman I'd ever seen in my life, plastered all over the covers." He pointed the knife towards me. "I saw you, Luke. You looked so sad and depressed. Sure, you were smiling in the photos, but I can read people better than anyone else can. I know sad and depressed. And when I saw how sad you were I knew you would be the perfect person to change my life around. You want to know how?"

My entire body was convulsing, not knowing what to do. Not knowing what the answer was.

"FUCKING ANSWER ME!"

I shook my head rigorously.

"Good girl. Always answer your husband. You respect me," he paused. "Now, where was I? Ah, yes! You were young, beautiful and *rich*. What more could a man want?" He smiled as if he were proud of himself. "I made a plan to get you to be mine. I changed my name, where I came from, what I did for a living. I changed everything about who I was, and I became the type of person I knew you would fall for." He gave a smug look. "Everything was going according to plan until your bitch of a mother and your friends started putting negative ideas about me in your head. But I guess plans don't always go the way you want them to. There's always something that seems to get in the way."

How in the hell did I not see what my parents and friends

saw in this guy? How could I not see that there was more than one side to this man? It was like he was a complete stranger and I *know* people can be blinded by love, but holy fuck! Every one of my senses seemed to be turned off when it came to him. Like I had rose colored glasses glued to my face. All I saw was a man who was everything I could've ever want and more. But now seeing him like this, this erratic, chaotic delusional person, I couldn't believe I was that dense to not see *one single* red flag. You would think someone following me around and staring at me would have been a dead giveaway. Not to me apparently.

"And now we find ourselves here," he gestured. "At this wonderful moment where I've decided that in order to stay aligned with my little plan, your parents need to go." He cocked his head. "I have *you*, Luke," he smiled. "Once everything gets cleared up and you get your inheritance, *then* we'll see what happens to you. I just need you to sign the checks, anyways," he briefly paused. "Oh! And to keep fucking me because I love doing that. Fucking you *fast* and *hard* until you cum. I know you like it too." He winked.

Anyways," he broke the eye contact he had on me and gestured towards my parents. "I was going to let you say your goodbyes, but I really don't want to hear their voices and I'm still pissed at you for interrupting me. So, I'm not going to take the tape off of you either."

My heart fell to my stomach realizing that this was it. This was the last time I was ever going to see my parents alive, *ever* again. I couldn't run up and hug them, or kiss them one last time. I couldn't tell them how much I loved them or how much they meant to me. I couldn't even thank them for giving me the life they did. I was their greatest creation and I had let them down. I had failed them.

My parents, my beautiful, wonderful, magical parents. I

could only look at them, look into their eyes and convey the love I had for them through the very thing that made them as extraordinary as they were.

I first looked at my father. I could tell he was telling me he loved me. And at the exact moment I was telling him, in my head, that I was sorry, he nodded once like he heard me.

When I looked at my mother, I had to blink a few times to clear the blurred vision from the tears that were beginning to pour from my eyes. I conveyed to her just how much I loved her and understood how much she loved me. I promised her that if I made it out of this alive, I would do something in honor of both of them. I would make something meaningful out of my life and I would make them proud of who I was.

I told her I loved her more than she would ever know and how I was thankful she was mother. My beautiful, extraordinary mother. When I looked at her for those last seconds, she was calmly nodding as if she understood me and was telling me she loved me back.

I put my head down, closed my eyes and deeply began to cry. That's when the most terrible thing I could've ever imagined seeing in my life happened. Mitch walked behind my parents and said, "Don't worry Luke, I'm all you need," before running the knife along each of their necks, slitting both of my parents' throats directly in front of me.

Chapter Ten

Forcefully holding my arm, Mitch dragged my depleted, listless body across the yard and back to the pool house. I knew that even if I could find it in me to put up a fight, he would hurt me. My energy was lost to the disbelief of what I had just witnessed. Not that it would matter. I was now faced with the reality where anything could happen and this was a position I put myself in. He had all the control and knew it. This had been his plan from the start. If I made any attempt at making a run for it, he would do something bad. Possibly even end me.

When we got to the door, I suddenly came back to reality as my attention turned to something I didn't notice when I had gotten home earlier. He had changed the locks. The key I once used with a Prada keychain my mother had given me would no longer work, or be needed. It would no longer be there, just like my mother. There was now a passcode I knew he wouldn't give me, and I knew wouldn't have any senti-mental meaning behind it. I think the reason I didn't notice before was because the note had been strategically covering it. I was too enthralled in the idea of my parents possibly accepting him, that I didn't notice. Thinking about it in hindsight, it was covering up the imminent change my life would now be facing.

As soon as we got through the door, Mitch threw me forcefully onto the couch. My hands were still tied behind my back so I couldn't catch myself as I landed on my side unable to sit upright. Lying there, feelings of anger and rage were coming to the surface, but I was unable to speak because the tape was still covering my mouth. Holding back the fight I wanted to let out made me realize I needed to be strategic with my own actions because with whatever was going to happen next, my brain would be my only hope in surviving this.

So, I went numb.

I stayed still, silent, where he'd thrown me, not wanting him to know I needed help.

When he noticed I couldn't sit up on my own, he rushed over to me. "Luke! Baby! I'm so sorry. Are you hurt? Are you in any pain?" His entire demeanor had changed.

I shook my head no, even though I *was* in pain. I was in the type of pain he couldn't see. It was internal. It was pain no one should ever experience. It was a pain in my heart that would *never* be mended.

"Here, let me take these off of you." He pulled a pocketknife out of his back pocket and cut the ties.

Now being freed, I knew being in the position I was in, I would have to go against my fight or flight instincts and play into a victim disposition as much as I didn't want to. I'd seen dateline. I'd read those kinds of books. I knew what to do.

I sat there, slumped over appearing to be a defeated woman. He sat down next to me on the couch looking me in my eyes before removing the tape like he was trying to read me. Tears were running down my cheeks from the cries I was letting out for my parents, but I knew I could use them to my advantage. I thrust myself onto him wrapping him tightly in an embrace as if he were the only one I needed.

He met my embrace with his. "See? Now you know why I had to do it. Aren't you happy? Don't you feel so much better?"

I let out a whimper of sadness from trying to hold in my cries, for my parents; the two people I loved most. I forced a nod to please him. He had just taken my *whole world* away from me, but I had to keep fighting for myself because I knew that's what my parents would have wanted.

He pulled me away from him, staring into my eyes like he did the first time I saw him. "Here, let me take this off of you."

I stretched my mouth, licking my lips, feeling the raw, exposed skin that had been pulled up from the tape. I wanted to scream at him. I wanted to hit him. To punch him. I wanted to ask him why? Because I didn't actually understand why he had to do what he did, but I stayed quiet. I let the rage I had towards him continue to build up.

"Aren't you happy, baby?" The way he said baby made me shudder. I felt disgusted that I'd ever let this man touch me, let alone put his lips on mine.

"Mmhmm," I nodded.

"Well, tell your face then." His voice, harsh.

I responded with a smile to appease him.

"There you go. There's my beautiful wife."

He got up from the couch and started to pace, causing my adrenaline to rise. I couldn't help but think, *what was he going to do next?*

I started to look around the room to see if I could reach for something to defend myself, but immediately noticed my things had been moved out of place. My little sanctuary I took so much pride in not only felt different now, but it also looked different as well.

"Oh, I see you've noticed." He said with smug confidence. "I had to put away anything that could be used as a weapon. You know, for *our* safety." He winked before walking back over to me and taking my hand as he sat down. "I want to talk to you about some ground rules now that we're married and free from, well, you know who."

I could've said something. I could've asked questions. I could've even tried to attack him. But silence fell over me once more not knowing where or what my words or actions could lead him to do to me. Would he hit me back? Or do something worse? I didn't want to find out. So, I just smiled and nodded as if everything were okay. As if what he did was completely normal.

"You're my wife. So, act like it." He was aggressive in his words. "I want you to be made up every day. I *never* want to see you not dressed or without makeup. You're not a whore, you're my wife." He paused for a slight second. "And I want all of my meals made and served to me on the dining room table. Breakfast, lunch and dinner. Tell me what you'll need, and *I'll* go out and buy it. Which reminds me, I'll need your pin number for your debit card." He ran his hand alongside my face to push some hair back that had fallen. "You're my wife and I expect you to treat me how a wife treats her husband. Do you understand me?"

I nodded.

"Tell me, what does that mean?"

My voice began to crack. "I'm your wife and need to do all of the normal wifely duties."

"Which are?" he pressed.

"To love," I paused. "Honor and . . ." The last one was harder to get out. "Obey you."

"And when you say love, what does that mean to you, Luke?" He asked condescendingly.

"To make love to you, my husband." I kissed him, reluctantly, on the cheek.

"Good girl. And when we make love, I want you to come on to me, to seduce me like a woman who wants to fuck her husband. You got that?"

"I do."

"Show me."

My breath was shaky as I rose to stand in front of the man I had fallen in love with, but now could barely recognize.

I slowly began to remove my top when he put his hand on my chest to stop me. "I said to *seduce* me."

Men were always so eager to sleep with me. I never had to do anything, but give in. I wasn't quite sure what to do. The men I ended up with wanted to make me happy, so I never paid much attention to getting them off. I was only focused on myself and what I wanted, or rather, *needed*.

The only time my body was ever in tune with another was when I was with Richie. Everything flowed together naturally, and it was because we genuinely loved and respected one another. But here, in this moment, where I had to prove something to my captor, my husband, I was at a loss for what to do.

I wasn't dumb though. I knew whatever I did would pass because men and woman think differently about sex. Women make an emotional connection whereas a man could get off by one little nip slip. So, I smiled at him, while dying a little more on the inside, before lowering myself down and starting to kiss his neck.

As I made my way down to his chest, I got down on my knees and proceeded to run my hands down his front until I got to his belt. I slowly unbuckled it before unzipping his jeans all while glaring at him, with full composure, into the eyes of a cold-hearted murderer.

He started to groan and move his body as the small amount of pleasure I was administering to him began to fulfill his needs. With every noise he emitted, vomit was ascending from my stomach wanting to expel itself all over him.

In hindsight, I should've bitten off his dick right then and there to end what I knew made him feel like a man. It would have been great. It wouldn't have been payback for taking my parents from me, but taking something important from him that would make him never feel the same again would have been satisfying.

I was too afraid though. Too afraid he would come after me and end my life the second he got the chance. So, I inevitably had to force myself to pleasure him. In doing so, it made me die *even more* inside.

"Now that's a good wife," he hummed after he finished. "That was fucking incredible."

It may have been everything to him, but I was left shaking in utter disbelief with myself that I was in a situation I never could've *ever* imagined. A thought flashed before my mind that my life was worth living, and right then that was how I was going to have to live it.

Chapter Eleven

That night I couldn't sleep. My mind kept racing, trying to think of all the ways I could escape this. Escape *him*. When I could hear the sound of his sleep, I snuck out of bed to text Remy what happened and for him to send help.

During the silent search for my purse, I mentally retraced my steps from the time I left The Polo Lounge to the time I got home. I remembered walking to my door and finding the note. Then my heart sank, remembering I had it when I was walking into my parents' house.

Knowing who he was now, Mitch had to have taken it away when I was passed out. He was clever. Evil, and clever, the worst combination.

A strange feeling crept in. A feeling I don't know how to explain. Fear? Survival? The need to protect myself? So, I started to look through every drawer in the house trying to find some sort of clue, or means to communicate. Something. Anything. But I was left frozen at the most bizarre sight.

I was standing in the kitchen staring at a once full drawer. All of the silverware, knives, sharp objects that could be used as a "weapon" were nowhere to be found. Panic came over me, in waves, as a true sense of fear began to set in as I realized that I may *not* actually get out of this. That realization was terrifying.

Being as cautious as I could to not wake him, I snuck back into bed lying there the entire night wide awake. He had me trapped for as long as he wanted me for himself, which felt like it could be forever. But how long is forever when you know forever could end at any moment?!

As the sun started to rise, I knew I needed to stay on his good side in order to stay alive. At least that's what I'd always heard. You're supposed to befriend your kidnapper, which was what I saw myself as; someone who was kidnapped, by their husband. Their murderous husband. It was some sort of sick, twisted reverse Stockholm syndrome where I was falling out of love with my captor. But I had to do whatever he wanted, whatever he asked.

I got out of bed and made myself presentable. Trying to get ready when your mind is racing is not as easy as it seems no matter how many times you've done your daily routine. Your mind is elsewhere, and you simply forget what you are doing. I fumbled with my lipstick, steadying my hands as best as I could. Taking deep breaths, in and out, before looking up at someone I hardly recognized in my reflection. I no longer saw Luke "Fucking" Townsend. I saw someone who had never truly known what it felt like to be broken. My old self was just a bandage covered version who played the "woe me" strings of the tiniest little violin. I thought the world was out to get me when really, I was the one out to get the world.

When I finished, I didn't know what to do, so the only thing I felt I could turn to for some sort of comfort, were my books. I wanted to escape and feel like I used to before I met Mitch Bellamy. My fingers grazed the spines before settling on one of my childhood favorites, The Secret Garden. As I began to read the words on the page an idea occurred to me. I could use these words, these beautifully written words, to form a message in case I was ever found.

Slowly, so I could be as silent as possible, I ripped different words and letters out of books to arrange them into sentences. Sitting there with the words before me, I glanced around wondering what I would do with them when his cleverness caught my eye once more.

He went as far as removing the glass from my picture frames. If he could think of a detail as minute as that, who knew what else he could conjure up? I quickly took apart the backing and arranged my messages. 'He kidnapped me.' 'He killed parents.' 'Help.'

I didn't know if they would ever be found, but the hope of knowing they could, made the rush of not getting caught a little calmer on my racing heart.

The only thing I could think to do was pray, and I'm not the praying kind of woman, but praying to whoever was up there listening, to somehow let someone figure out what happened, made my belief in something greater, strong. I left little one-word messages for my friends hidden behind books and in drawers hoping Mitch would never find them. *Help. Lost. Save.* That was my way of still feeling connected to the real world. It was my way of having . . . faith.

Mitch walked out of the bedroom towards me on the couch, presentable, reading a book like the bored 1950's housewife he wanted me to be. "Well, look at that," he smiled. "Look at my beautiful wife, ready and waiting for her husband." He walked over and kissed me on the cheek.

"Good morning, Mitch. How did you sleep?" I put on the

perfect act, just like he wanted, although inside I was retching with disgust for him.

"After last night, I slept like a baby thanks to you."

"I'm glad, honey," I smiled. "I always want to make you feel like the *big, strong* man that you are." I stood up, putting my arms around him like I was the perfect, fucking, stepford wife. I was just missing the apron. "Now, what can I make you for breakfast?"

"Hmmm, how about some eggs and bacon," he answered.

"Perfect! Let me start on that." I gently caressed his chest, giving him a coy little look before walking to the kitchen where I immediately changed my expression once he couldn't see my face. I pulled the eggs and bacon out of the fridge and headed towards the cabinets to grab a bowl. When I reached for the silverware drawer to get a fork, I knew wasn't there, I played dumb and asked, "Huh. Honey? Do you happen to know where the silverware is? I seem to have misplaced them."

"Oh no, that was my doing, sweetie. We can't afford to have any little mishaps in this plan." He walked over to where I was. "I thought I told you last night. I removed anything that could be used as a weapon against me."

"Oh, right. I'm sorry. It slipped my mind after pleasuring you last night. That's all I can think about." I let out a little giggle, a gesture very unlike me.

He grabbed my ass pulling me into him squeezing it tightly. My breathing started to shake, afraid he was going to hurt me, but instead he whispered, "What do I always tell you? A beautiful woman should never have to apologize."

I forced a smile trying to release the tensed state my body went into when he grabbed me.

"That's my fucking wife." He kissed me on the neck.

"Maybe we should put breakfast off for a bit. I want *you* first."

I drove myself right into that one and quickly made a mental note to watch what I said.

I cried, standing in the bathroom, staring at my reflection in the mirror, again not recognizing the woman I had become in the past 24 hours. I was no longer the woman people wanted to be. The woman who was once envied and fawned after. I felt so stupid. I was now the kind of woman I didn't really know even existed until I was experiencing a different side of life I had always put a blind eye to.

How could I have not seen right through him? I could usually see right through anyone.

The pressure in my chest, from the scream I was holding in, made it feel like I couldn't breathe. It hadn't even been a full day and it was already taking everything in me to not break down and completely lose my shit. There weren't any words in the English language that would communicate exactly how I was feeling. Rage and fury were low on the totem pole of emotions I had. They were words which now had little connotation to what I was feeling inside. But I had to keep whatever this new feeling was down, so I could continue to try and live.

After I composed myself, I walked back into the kitchen to find a few utensils laid out on the countertop. Mitch was sitting at the table smiling as he watched my every move and I mean *every* move.

His stare bore into me as I scrambled the eggs. Nerves rattling my insides with fake composure on the outside, reflecting in my precise movements making sure his breakfast was cooked to his liking. Fear, looming over my head, that if I made a mistake, he would kill me.

I sat there looking at him after serving him his plate. My appetite had been lost the moment he took my parents away from me. As I sat there in silence, listening to the sounds of his eating, my stomach started to churn. In the silence I could hear his every bite, every chew and every scrape of the fork against the plate. It was disgusting. Nauseating. Rage inducing.

"Aren't you going to eat?" he gestured towards the plate in front of me.

"Oh, I'm not very hungry. I think I'll just wait until lunch," I replied bringing my plate to the sink.

"I like that you're watching your figure for me. I'd like my wife to stay sexy."

My jaw clenched holding back the tears wanting to pour from my eyes and the scream still filling my chest. I coerced a smile and turned around. "Of course! I just want to make you happy, Mitch." I walked back towards him and sat down. I was quiet for a moment before mustering up the courage to test the waters. "Oh honey, I promised Margot I would lend her my vintage Gucci scarf for a wedding she's attending this weekend. Would I be able to call her to have her swing by sometime today to pick it up?"

The rattling of the plate startled me more than his fist slamming on the table. "Luke, I'm sorry. I didn't mean to scare you."

"Well, that was uncalled for Mitch." I crossed my arms and turned away hoping my acting was convincing enough.

"Listen, baby." He got up and kneeled down next to me. "I want you for myself. Your friends are going to have to wait a while to see you. Don't worry, I'll text Margot and tell her you don't feel well and can't find the scarf."

"But I promised her, and I never break my promises to my friends." I turned towards him, tears of defeat filling my eyes.

"Listen, I'll take care of it." I leaned into his hand as it caressed the side of my face.

"Okay. Thank you."

Later that night, he took things to a level of extreme discomfort I wouldn't wish upon anyone.

I wanted to take a shower and shave my legs. Knowing how smart he was, I knew the razor wouldn't be where I usually kept it. So, I asked, "Mitch? May I please have my razor? I'd like to shave my legs."

Nothing would've ever prepared me for just how uncomfortable it is to have someone sit there watching you shave your legs with the shower door open. If it was Margot, it would have been different. If it was even Remy or Franklin, it would have been different. If it was Mitch, before everything happened, it would have been different. But when it's someone you're afraid of, it makes you feel exposed and vulnerable in the worst of ways.

My hands were shaking, making my strokes staggered instead of smooth. And when I accidentally nicked myself, he snapped. "Be more careful, Luke. We've talked about this." His soulless, beady eyes glared through me. "Don't cut yourself, Luke. Pay more attention. I want you to be clean and damage free."

Then the thing which made me completely change the way I'd let anyone ever touch me again happened. He snatched the razor out of my hand and proceeded to finish shaving my legs for me. I held my breath, feeling violated in a way I didn't know was possible. I felt as though I were being groomed by someone for their own liking. Like he was making me his picture perfect, Luke.

It's something I'll never forget. The feeling of being a trophy or prized possession to someone who was capable of much more evil than I had ever seen in the world. It's something that will haunt me forever.

Chapter Twelve

We've now come to another part of my story where I was not present for the events taking place. I was told all of this after this nightmare that happened to me, to all of us, was over. This is also where I will forever be grateful to the people who I have trusted and loved in my life. To the people who I *chose* to be my family. I will love them and cherish them more than they will ever know, until the day I die.

~

"Hey Remy, It's Margot. I just got the weirdest text from Luke."

"What did it say?"

"It says she can't find the scarf she said I could borrow for a wedding, so she can't lend it to me. Did we talk about scarves yesterday at dinner? I know I had a few glasses of champagne but not *that* many that I wouldn't remember."

"No, I didn't hear any talk about a scarf. That *is* weird," he paused. "You know what? She usually texts me when she gets home. You all do."

"That's because you make us."

"It's because I care," he emphasized. "She didn't text me last night."

"Well, she's married now, right? Even if it is to some creep we don't even know. I wanted to tell her *so* badly yesterday that Mitch isn't who he says he is. God it was terrible."

"I know, I saw the look on your face."

"I should've told her."

"No! Orson and Carter told us not to. I mean, I wanted to tell her too. I wanted to throw her in my car and take her to my place. Lock her inside until we can figure out how to get rid of this guy. But we just have to play it cool and do what the Townsend's tell us to do."

"This is brutal. She's our friend. I don't get it. Why won't she listen to us?"

"Because she's in love. She's like, blinded by his charm. I mean for someone who's such a snake, he *is* one charming son of a bitch."

"Have you talked to Franklin since last night?"

"Yes, he texted me!"

Margot scoffed.

"He thought dinner was weird too. Agrees that we need to keep things as is as if we have no idea what we really know about the situation."

"This fucking sucks."

"I know. But what can we do?"

A few days passed from that initial phone call, but my friends, Margot, Remy and Franklin continued on with their normal lives. What my normal life used to look like.

Apparently, during that time, Remy had gotten a few texts from me. They were normal pleasantries of 'hellos' and 'how are you's?' There was even a text telling him I was just spending some time with Mitch so I wouldn't be on my phone much. One of them even went as far as telling Remy how we were thinking about starting a family and possibly moving. The messages seemed a little off to him, and didn't sit right.

"Has Luke been texting you guys?"

"She just sent a 'what's up' text," Franklin said. "Nothing out of the ordinary, but it was phrased in a weird way. That's the only thing I found a little odd."

"Oh my god! Same, here. I mean, like, after that weird scarf text I asked her if she was okay or needed anything. She wrote back that she was fine and was in so much 'bliss' with Mitch," Margot gagged. "Yuck! And to not check in on them because they were off 'enjoying each other.' So gross. I don't know how she can even touch that man, let alone kiss him. Or even have sex with him. Eww," she shivered.

"Yeah, I noticed her texts were off too. Very unlike her. You know how grammatically correct she is."

"Yeah, it's nauseating," Margot rolled her eyes.

"Well, it's just unlike her." Remy thought to himself for a moment. "Do you think he's like, I don't know, drugging her or something?"

"That guy?" Franklin laughed. "No, way. He may be weird, stares a lot and is eerily quiet, but there's *no way* he would even be the type."

Margot raised her brow. "It's always the quiet ones."

"Maybe we're just too invested in this and we're trying to find things that are wrong," Remy suggested.

"No. Intuition is intuition and mine says this guy is a little off. *Especially* because his name isn't even fucking Mitch Bellamy," Franklin said matter-of-factly.

"Yeah, you're right. I'm just trying to find some sort of positive outlook here."

"Well, what have her parents said? They haven't texted or called me in a while. Have they contacted you?" Margot looked to Remy.

"Actually, no. I've texted them quite a few times and tried calling, but it's gone straight to voicemail." Remy paused before giving Franklin and Margot a worried look. "Do you guys think we should go over there and like, check in on them?"

"I don't see why not? It's not out of the ordinary for us to just drop by. Luke knows that," Franklin assured.

"Okay, should we go over now?" Remy looked to the both of them.

"Why not? I don't see anything new for me to buy in here anyways," Margot said, putting down a handbag she already owned.

My friends drove over to my house and upon pulling into the driveway, they noticed the landscape had been unkempt for what looked like days. Knowing me, and my parents, they knew how meticulous my mother was about keeping it up even though she wasn't always there. It was because of her "visual eye," she'd always say.

The three of them went to the main house first and rang the doorbell. After a few minutes of no one answering, they knocked. After a few more minutes of, yet again, no one answering, they decided to check the pool house. *My* house.

"Look," Margot pointed. "All of the curtains are drawn. Are they even here?"

"Maybe not. Maybe they're in New York for an opening," Franklin suggested.

"I don't think they would leave Luke knowing what we do. Not for anything," Remy added.

This next little part, I was there for, but they had no idea.

I was reading a book on the couch when I heard someone approaching. I felt an illuminated rush of happiness and relief thinking someone was here who could save me. It had been a week locked inside without any contact from the real world. Mitch had hidden the television remotes and laptop in my safe which he conveniently changed the code to. I had no way of getting help or even knowing if anyone was looking for me.

I jolted up, ready to bang on the windows and door, ready to scream and beg for my life. I was ready for them to save me.

Just as I was about to let out my life saving yell, Mitch came up from behind putting a knife to my neck and his hand over my mouth. "If you try anything funny or make even the *slightest* bit of noise, I'll slice your throat like I did your parents," he whispered.

So, I stood there.

Frozen.

Silent.

Hearing the familiar voices of my friends on the other side of the door made me crumble with defeat; knowing help was already gone when it had only just arrived. They were so close, yet so far.

"That's strange. When did she change the locks?" Remy asked. Of course, Remy would notice something like that. He was my protector. He was all of our protectors. He was kind-hearted and loyal. The *best* friend you could ever ask for. He was the type of friend who only wanted the best for you, for *me*.

"This is too weird. It's unsettling." Margot, my beautiful Margot. She had a heart of gold even though you would only think it was made of ice. She and I had a love hate kind of relationship. We bickered like sisters, but at the end of the day we would always be there for one another with nothing but love and support. She was a part of my chosen family, after all. And although she was self-centered, deep down she cared for everyone around her. She just had a funny way of showing it.

"What about their housekeeper?" Franklin suggested. "Maybe she can let us in and we can see if anything looks weird or out of place on the inside." My smart, noble Franklin, always thinking outside the box and shocking you with it when you least expected it. He was the one who'd listen when you needed to cry. He was the one who'd hold you until you felt better. My Franklin. My sweet, sweet Franklin.

These were the people, my people, who were going to save my life. I knew it. I believed it because I believed in them. But as I continued to stand there, silently crying, Mitch's hand still covering my mouth, feeling the cool touch of the blade against my throat, a rush of calm fell over me. A weight lifted, feeling that no matter what happened, there were people out there who actually cared about me and loved me. I don't know why I hadn't seen it before. I was too traumatized by losing the two people I loved most in the world just a few days prior, and the two others, two years before that I didn't realize my friends were really the only ones I needed. They had been there for *everything* and would be there for me now because they *knew* me. And they knew something wasn't right.

When I heard them walking away, my heart fell to the pit of my stomach. All of the hope I had was walking away with them.

Mitch, knife still at my throat, brought me over to the door. He looked through the peep hole and saw they were walking back to the main house. "Fuck! They messed everything up. I should've done to them what I did to your parents. FUCK!" He threw the knife to the floor along with me into the wall.

I was left shaking, feeling like my only chance of being saved was lost.

"Okay, okay, I have to think," he muttered to himself.

Margot, Remy and Franklin went back to the front door of my parents' house and tried ringing the doorbell once more.

They were left with disappointment again.

They didn't know what to do. They just knew they couldn't give up on finding my parents. On finding me.

Remy then remembered our housekeeper also worked for an ex-boyfriend of his, so he called him to get her number.

"Hi Amelia! This is Remy, Luke's friend. We're at the Townsend's home right now and no one's answering. We have a really bad feeling that something might be wrong. Do you know if they might've gone somewhere?"

"Oh, yes! Mr. Bellamy told me last week how they were all flying to Europe for a few months for a gallery opening. He said I didn't need to come clean, as they would be gone, but I would still get paid. I thought it was a little strange because whenever they are gone, I make sure the house is okay and nothing goes wrong while they're away. Like a leak or anything. He insisted that I don't come and should enjoy my time off. He said a friend of his was going to come and check on the house for them. I told him I would have to double check with Mr. and Mrs. Townsend, but he said they were stressed about the opening and had asked him if he could take care of all the arrangements. Usually, Mrs. Townsend tells me months before an opening. She didn't tell me about this one."

"Yeah, we don't think there is one. Would you be able to come over here as soon as you can and let us in? We feel like something's off. We had no idea about Europe either. Luke never mentioned that to us and from her texts, it seems like she's still here."

"Yes, okay. I can be there in about thirty minutes. I'm not too far away."

"Thank you, Amelia, we'll see you soon."

When Amelia arrived, she got out of her car and noticed the landscape as well. "I guess he told the landscapers not to come either. Wow! This is so unlike the Townsends."

"That's what we think too. We're worried something's wrong," Margot said.

As they were walking to the front door Remy stopped. "Should we call the police for this?"

"I mean, we have the key. Can't we just go in? We're friends, basically family," Franklin replied.

"I have a bad feeling about this." Margot looked to them.

Amelia pulled out the key and held it displayed in her hand. "Well, I'm allowed to go in, but I'm scared. *He* scares me. He isn't a good a man. He's not good for Luke. Mrs. Townsend always says you can tell who someone is from their eyes, and he's not good."

"He scares all of us." Margot put her arm around Amelia.

"Okay, how about we all go in together? That works, right? I mean, it's probably nothing, but there's power in numbers. At least I hope there is." Remy tried to bring some light to the situation, he was being the protector.

"Oh my god! What's that smell?" Margot gagged.

Covering his nose and mouth Remy replied, "I don't know but I might throw up! Oh god! Why is it so hot in here?"

"I think we should call the cops," Franklin said, panicked. "Something's wrong, something's really wrong."

Even though the smell was unbearable, they still walked in to see if they could find where it was coming from. When they walked into the formal living room, they saw them.

Margot started screaming. Remy started to throw up. Amelia fell to the floor crying, and Franklin dialed 911.

"Help! Help! You have to come. We just found our best

friend's parents murdered in their home. Please hurry! It's Orson and Carter Townsend."

When the paramedics got there, they told everyone to go outside. The police arrived shortly after.

My friends told the police everything they knew about Mitch, including his real name and how they never trusted him. They told them how my parents had hired a private investigator and how they were going to try and get me away from him. When they hadn't heard from my parents in a week, and my texts were out of character for what they were used to hearing, they decided to come and check on us. The four of them were told to calm down and that everything would be figured out. They had nothing to do but put faith in the police that not only would Mitch be caught, because they knew it was him, but that I would be found. Alive.

Chapter Thirteen

Mitch thought of a plan almost immediately. He had a few planned out in case something like this were to happen. At least, that's what I found out later.

"You have two minutes to stuff whatever shit you can into this bag."

Stumbling backwards from him shoving a bag into me, I began frantically looking around as though I were in a panic. I wanted it to appear like I was ready to flee with him; like I actually wanted to go. All I could think about was getting my friends' attention so they knew to come running to my aide.

My movements were manic, knocking things over with the bag as I "searched" for things to pack, purposely knocking over the picture frame with the hidden message for someone to, hopefully, find.

It was a bizarre situation to be in, forcing myself to be frantic, on the brink of an anxiety attack, all to allude him into believing I was on his side, ready to run away with him. He knew there was a possibility of the end of us. The end of him.

This was too close. He felt like he had been caught. I

could see it in his reaction and his movements around the house. He was in a constant state of thinking. Bewildered in his own mind, trying to gather everything he thought he needed for the next venture out into a world he thought he could get away free and clear in.

My breathing became rapid; the anxiety attack I was faking becoming real not knowing what to do but hoping somehow my friends were still on the grounds where I could get their attention.

I had to do something, anything, to try and get him to stop for a second and distract him from what was swirling around in his mind. I had to stall him.

"What should I pack?" I stressed. "Should I bring dresses? Heels? Bikini's? What type of weather should I be packing for Mitch? Where are we going?"

"Pack something that won't make you stand out," he snapped.

I did the exact opposite and packed everything that would.

"What about my makeup and hair products? Should I bring those? Everything won't fit in this bag. And I can't leave without my jewelry. I . . ."

"God damn it, Luke! I know what you're fucking doing. Just go to the door, we have to hurry," he yelled.

"But Mitch, what about my things?" I pleaded.

He walked up to me grabbing my hair from behind, yanking it back with force. "You won't need anything. You only need me, remember?"

"Yes, I remember."

"Good girl," he released his grip. "Listen, I have a car stashed down the street a ways. We're going to sneak out through the back hedges behind the tennis court. If you make *any* noise," he pointed the knife he'd thrown to the ground only moments before towards me. "Try to run away from me, or signal for help in any way, I *will* kill you right then and there. Do you understand me?"

"Yes. Okay, I won't do anything, Mitch. I promise." I meant it. I wasn't ready to die yet. I'd never wanted to live more in my life than in that moment.

My friends had to have been just yards away, on the front side of the main house. I could have gotten their attention. I knew I could have. One little scream. One little cry for help. It would have been so easy. And although he was *making* it easy to want to get out of this, there was a part of me that felt like I wouldn't be able to.

"Give me your hands."

"Why?" I questioned.

"For insurance." He started to zip tie my wrists together. "I don't completely trust you."

"Mitch," I said, somberly.

"What?" He met my eyes with his.

"I love you," I whispered.

He glared at me. I could tell he was contemplating if I meant it or not. The questions of my deception flooded his face as his eyes narrowed.

But my face remained soft.

It's hard to convince yourself to convey love for a man standing before you when you only love the man you once knew him to be. A man who's now, gone.

"I love you too," he finally broke the silence. "We're going to get away from here and be together forever. I promise, I'm going to protect you, Luke. You're *mine*."

"I know. I believe you," I lied. "I just want to be with you too."

His cold, chilling lips met mine with a kiss. Any and all passion or feelings of love and desire, which were once there, were completely dead. Long gone. Just like the man I once knew. He was a stranger to me now, and someone I wished I'd never met.

"Can I trust you to not scream or make any noise?"

"Yes, Mitch. I promise."

"Okay. Then I won't put tape over your mouth."

"Thank you," I whispered, running my tongue over the lips that had just healed from the last time he ripped tape from my mouth.

He turned, blocking me from view of the passcode while he entered it. "Okay, move," he said pulling me to the front of him where he then started to guide me from behind, pushing me down the path to the tennis court. My head looked forward, but my eyes scanned the grounds, hoping to see my friends. *Someone. Anyone.*

I had once heard, or read somewhere, that if someone takes you and you're in a populated space, if you try to get away when they've threatened to kill you, they won't actually do it. I didn't know if this would be the case here. We were in my own home, on my own property. Even if we did see someone, it wouldn't be a crowd. It would be one of my friends, a landscaper or maintenance person. So, would he really kill me? There would be a witness, but he would probably kill them too.

Everything in me wanted to scream. I wanted to turn around and punch him in the stomach or kick him in the balls. I was so afraid that he wouldn't be the way I'd read him. He was too up and down where the new version of himself, his real self, was unpredictable from one moment to the next. Maybe he *would* actually kill me. After all, I only knew the made-up version of him. *Mitch.* I didn't know the version who was his true identity, *Jason.*

As I scanned the property, I saw things I could easily use

to hurt him, possibly even kill him with. He wasn't someone I loved anymore. He was someone I hated. I could do it. I could kill him. I could turn this around and give him a taste of his own medicine.

My thoughts were too mixed up, not knowing what this man would and wouldn't do to me. I had seen what he was capable of, but was there a little part of him that wasn't capable of doing it to me? Was there a little part of him, deep down inside, that was still Mitch?

Because if he were Mitch, I could question whether or not I'd want to hurt him. My reasoning being Mitch would never want to hurt me. I knew that. I felt that.

The second my mother had said his real name, it triggered something in him causing him to revert back from the invented version of himself to his true self. To the man he'd always been and never wanted to be. His true identity.

In my heart I knew Mitch. Even though my parents and friends could see what I couldn't, I knew him. I knew he was gentle and kind and in love with me. But now I was seeing the evil they warned me about firsthand. Being on this side of his personality, I had truly begun to realize how I had no idea who this man was and exactly what I was dealing with.

I was so back and forth in my own mind. Lost in a constant battle of feelings and emotions, I kept contemplating if I should just risk it. There wouldn't be much to lose. My parents were gone and although I loved my friends, life would go on for them if I wasn't in it. They could still live. If there was a possibility that I would even get out of the situation I was in, my life would be different. Maybe if I tested the waters a little, I could see what he was capable of doing to someone he supposedly loved. I knew Mitch loved me, but did Jason?

When I finally worked up the courage to try, I couldn't

get any type of sound out. My voice was frozen, locked as if I never even knew how to speak. The only thing I could do was continue to play into him, into what he was believing to be reality. My way of thinking quickly became clear. I had to be strategic and knew I had to keep making him think I wanted him, and I was going to do whatever it took to make him believe I was on his side. Trust was a major factor. I had to make him trust me, but it's hard to make someone trust you when you don't trust them.

"Get in the back, lay down, shut up and cover yourself up with that blanket."

"Okay." I did what he asked, leaving a small opening for me to be able to breath. But suddenly, the urge to take a chance came over me. Maybe it would open up an opportunity for me to figure out how to escape. "Where are we going?"

"I'll let you know when you can uncover yourself. Until then, shut the fuck up so I can think."

I lay under the blanket, afraid to move, for what felt like forever. I had already made him mad, if I brought that anger out of him now there'd be no telling what he would do. So, I stayed quiet, listening to the sound of the wheels rolling against the pavement. Passing cars made me wonder where we could even be heading. We kept stopping and going so I knew we were in traffic that much I could tell. Canada? Mexico? There were endless possibilities really. It seemed easy enough to get lost someone. But where?

Mitch kept muttering nonsense to himself every time he slammed the brakes. "Fuck you bitch! Hurry the fuck up! God, these fucking people can't drive."

Then there would be moments of silence which were soon broken by his own words of encouragement.

"You're doing fine . . . Everything's fine . . . They won't

be able to find you in this car . . . You're going to get away. You've got this, Jason."

The sound of him calling himself by his real name made my heart drop. Absolute disgust filled my stomach and I had to take slow, deep breaths in order to not vomit.

"We'll get there, and I'll think of my next move. I'll think of what to do with her, and I'll get away. I'll fucking get away and all this shit will be over."

My imagination started to run wild, thinking of every possible scenario. Maybe we'd run away together to a different country and start a different life together, or apart. Maybe I'd somehow manage to get away, unscathed, turning him into the police and getting the justice my parents deserved. Maybe he'd leave me somewhere letting me be free all on his own. Would I turn him in? Or would I be too afraid that maybe, like in a movie, he'd threaten me, leaving me to live the rest of my life constantly looking over my shoulder. Then my mind drifted to the worst possible scenario. Maybe this was my last day. Maybe these were my last few hours, alive.

Chapter Fourteen

From what I could tell, we were on the freeway by the way we had suddenly started to cruise at a steady pace when he finally spoke to me. "You can get out of there now."

I tore the blanket from myself, breathing in the cool air, trying to focus my eyes against the blinding light of the sun. For some reason, I had a newfound bit of courage in me. "Where are we going?"

"Climb up front and sit next to me so it doesn't look suspicious." He ignored my question. "But if you try anything, I'll kill you right here." He gestured to the knife he held in his hand.

"Okay." I made my way up front, my hands still zip-tied together making note of the Volvo logo on the steering wheel and the dated dashboard.

He shoved a bottle of water towards me. "Here's some water if you're thirsty."

I uncapped it and took a sip.

He made the situation confusing. At times he was sweet and compassionate as if he were the Mitch I knew, the Mitch

I fell in love with, but at other times he was erratic and chaotic, much like how he was the other night when he killed my parents. I was starting to believe he was mentally unstable. Someone diagnosed with multiple personalities or was even diagnosed as bipolar. All I knew was I had to keep pleasing him. I had to keep his ego thinking, or rather believing, I was on his side. "Thank you, that was really sweet of you."

"Luke, you're my wife. I'm going to take care of you." His tone, harsh, made him seem genuine but at the same time all the more, frightening.

"I know. It's just really nice to feel like you're taking care of me," I told him, trying to keep him in a mind fuck of his own. I extended my hand for him to hold, and he met it with a squeeze.

My emotions were perplexed. Having to act a certain way was making me lose the strength I thought I once had. I played the part of Luke "Fucking" Townsend so well I actually started to believe I was her. But I wasn't. I was a girl who'd be happier with her head stuck in a book living in the imaginations of others through the words transcribed before me. All I knew was being alone, lost in the worlds I read about. The only people I could truly be myself around were my parents and Richie. They were the only three people who understood me because I could be honest with them. They let me be Luke; just Luke. Not this made-up version of myself I portrayed for others.

Yes, I absolutely adored my friends, but I put up my act for them. We weren't the same, but I believed in myself so much, in what I was portraying for them, that I became who they saw. I wish I had told them my little secret instead of only showing them the dumbed down version I wanted them to see. It had become a regret of mine seeing as I had all the time in the world to reflect on my life. I should've shown them who I really was and if they didn't accept it, it would have been on them.

My reinventions were masks hiding myself from who I truly was. They were pleasing everyone else instead of pleasing the one person who truly mattered most in my life. Me. I let myself become arrogant. I let myself become a bitch. All because I was trying to fit this mold of who people thought I should be. There I was, doing it again. Pretending to still love Mitch as a means for survival, but I was believing it so much so that my head and heart couldn't decipher what was reality and what was an act. Yes, I was frightened of him. I hated him. But I still felt like a part of me, deep down inside, was still in love with him.

"Now, don't you see why your parents had to go? They were trying to break us apart. This, right here." He emphasized our linked hands with a firm shake. "They never understood what true love and sacrifice was. This," he brought my hand to his mouth meeting it with a kiss. "What we have, is more real than anything I could *ever* see in a movie. We're it, baby. You and me."

I smiled in agreement, although I was feeling completely gutted inside. "So, what's our plan?" I made it a point to let him know I was included in what he had in store for us. It was important for him to feel like I would always be with him, even though on the inside I was trying to think of ways to escape him.

"We'll be in San Diego in a few hours, depending on traffic. We'll get a motel somewhere close to the border. In the morning we're going into Mexico. Then figure it out from there."

"That's a good plan, Mitch. I like it! We can definitely get lost there and create new identities. Maybe even make it all the way to Panama!" I said with excitement, hoping he'd match my false enthusiasm all while trying to give him more ideas to prove he could trust me, and not have the need to kill me. Silently thinking how maybe it would be a good idea to get lost so I could become who I really was. There was no one left to miss me.

"Luke, you're brilliant! That's why I married you," he paused. "God, when you're thinking you're so fucking sexy. Has anyone ever told you that before?"

Yes, Richie, but when he said it, I fell into his arms, and we made love. He didn't make me want to vomit. As for everyone else in my life, they were probably either too afraid, too intimidated, or didn't really care when I said something they deemed unexpected because I was the envy of the world. Everything I said or did was deemed great in their eyes.

"No," I shook my head. "You're the first."

"Well, it's true. God, fuck!" he yelled.

"What?"

"I want you so fucking bad right now."

"Why don't we pull over and get a hotel room around here?" If we were closer to L.A., it would be easier for someone to find me.

"No, we can't. We have to keep going. We can't stop. Here, come here." He reached for the back of my head.

"What are you doing?" I resisted.

"What do they call it? Road head?"

"Mitch!" I exclaimed, seemingly appalled at his suggestion. And I was.

I didn't want to be intimate with him. Although I felt like I was still in love with him in the warped way I was, I didn't see him in *that* way anymore. The idea of him touching me in such a familiar, intimate, way had my skin crawling.

"Come on Luke, make your husband happy," he pleaded, aggressively.

He wasn't this fascinated with sex when he was the Mitch he was portraying. This Jason, who he really was, was aggressive in all aspects of his behavior and demeanor. The thought of giving him what he wanted was vile to me. I didn't want to. I *really* didn't want to. *If you want to survive, do what he wants,* kept repeating in my head with dread filling my heart. So, I did it. And I felt ashamed and disgusted the entire time.

We drove in silence after. My insides trembling with disgust and hatred for the man who used to be my, everything. The deafening silence made the drive seem much longer than it actually was.

By the time we arrived at a motel, it was dark out. I wasn't familiar with San Diego as I'd only been a few times. I didn't know if we were close to the border, but could only assume we were.

"Stay in the car. I'm going to check-in." He turned back, narrowing his eyes before lifting himself out of the car. "And don't even *think* about trying anything fucking funny. *Everything* points to you." He wielded the knife in my face. "Actually," he paused. "Give me your hands."

"But I'm still tied together."

He let out his frustration with a heavy sigh as he forcefully grabbed my already tied together hands and zip tying me to the seatbelt.

Instead of feeling helpless and letting my captor, my husband, win in whatever game he was playing, I took the opportunity to try and get the upper hand. As soon as he was out of sight, I rummaged about the car as best I could using the parts of my body that were free; my legs, feet and even my hands by extending the seatbelt outward. I was hoping to find a cellphone, another knife, a gun, anything I could use against him. But I knew not to underestimate him. He was smart and knew what he was doing. This wasn't something he'd just come up with. He'd planned it and worked out every detail. So, even if he didn't act as if he were ten steps ahead, I knew he was. Mitch seemed to be the ploy and Jason, the complete, insane mastermind.

I sat there defeated, head hung low, the restraints holding me back from searching any further. This was it, almost like it were the end of the road. I had to come to terms with this being my fate. I would be paying back my karmic debt for not listening to the people who loved me the most. I brought the person who killed them into our lives. It was me and this was how it was going to end.

Just as those fleeting thoughts were leaving my mind and I was back to feeling a nothingness I was now feeling comforted by, the sound of moving gravel had me retreat to an upright position as another car pulled up beside me. The feeling of hope began to rise up from deep down inside once more.

It was dark and the dim lighting in the parking lot made me unsure if they would even be able to see me. This was my chance though, my opportunity to free myself. I was about to yell when a reflection from my peripheral caught my eye. Mitch was walking out of the office, and when he noticed the car, he started to pick up his pace.

My heart sank. *What could I do? What could I do?* Then I remembered I'd once seen a video on social media of a woman who had been kidnapped. She made a signal with her hands to let people know she needed help. I brushed it off, scoffing, thinking I'd never need to know that because it would never happen to me. Here's a lesson from someone who once thought too highly of themselves, *always remember the important things,* even if you never think you'll use them.

I didn't remember.

Mitch opened the door and I sat there facing forward in silence. "Good girl."

I acknowledged him then faced forward again. When I did, I was met with the eyes of a little girl, no more than 6 or 7, staring directly at me. This time, I *knew* she could see me because the light had turned on when Mitch opened the door. I sat there, frozen, trying to use the *one thing* my mother felt could convey the most to people, my eyes.

Without making any movements, I *pleaded* to the little girl to get help, to even just tell her parents something seemed off. But she was young. She wouldn't know what to do. She wouldn't know how to help or even know what to say. She was just a child. When my hope fleeted again, she did it. She tugged on her mother's arm and pointed at me. Her mother shooed her off as mother's do sometimes. She probably assumed her daughter was making something up, as children do. They walked into their room, and I closed my eyes feeling defeated by fate once more.

Mitch tugged at my hands cutting the zip ties with his knife. He gripped me tightly around my bicep and led me to our room. His grip grew tighter with every step. "I'm proud of you, Luke."

"For what?"

"For listening to your husband and not trying to get away," he paused. "That's how I know you really love me."

I wanted to rip his throat out but instead I gave him a shallow smile. "Yeah," I whispered. "I do."

Nothing had ever felt more like a lie, more depressing,

even lonelier, than to have to be here with this man I once loved and had to feed him what he wanted to hear. A part of me felt like I could stick this out, however long it would take to get rescued, but an even bigger part of me wanted to give up and let him end my life. It had come to that point. I had made my mistake and now I had to pay for it.

Chapter Fifteen

The sound of his zipper caught my attention, and I immediately went into a state of panic. I didn't want it to happen. I didn't want to do it. I couldn't let it happen.

Just as I was about to turn and face my imminent fate, Mitch pulled a long rope from his bag.

"Sit on the bed," he demanded.

I didn't hesitate. I sat on the bed knowing this would be better than what I thought was going to happen. He started to wrap the rope around my right ankle, tying me to the leg of the nightstand. As he stood up, he reached for the remote. Every move was done with intention.

Once the screen clicked on, there we were, plastered on every news channel. There would be no denying or hiding who we were, especially me. The media was trying to make a spectacle out of my parents' murder with me being the center of it.

"Orson and Carter Townsend, beloved artists and friends in the entertainment industry were found slain in their Beverly Hills home this evening by friends of their daughter, Luke Townsend-Bellamy, who is missing along with her husband, Mitch Bellamy. As of right now, they are the prime persons of interest in the case."

"Yes, Michelle, that's right. We're out in front of the Townsend residence here in Beverly Hills, where distraught family, friends and neighbors have gathered to mourn the loss of their friends who were not only loved and cherished in their community, but by the world."

"Thank you, Richard. Now, what can you tell us has happened so far?"

"From what we've learned on the scene, they were discovered this evening when friends of their daughter, Luke Townsend-Bellamy, came to check on them after not hearing from her for a few days. They were unable to get into the house, so they called the Townsends' housekeeper to let them in and that's when they made the tragic discovery. From what we've heard, they've been deceased for several days now and there's no sign of their daughter or son-in-law anywhere. Which is why they are of interest to be found. Her friends are worried something could've possibly happened to her as well, and seem to be pointing the finger towards the husband. We have overheard some rumblings from some of the people who've been standing by since the police first arrived on the scene, but we aren't allowed to give that information out just yet. All we know is that Luke Townsend-Bellamy and her husband, Mitch Bellamy, are missing and as of right now, it is a top priority to find their whereabouts. Back to you in the studio."

"FUCK!"

"Mitch, don't yell, someone could hear you." I stressed, even though I *did* want someone to hear him. I wanted someone to hear how manic he was. I wanted someone to come and break down the door. But if someone actually did come knocking on our door, what would that mean for me? Would I end up dead? Or alive? "Don't worry, we'll figure this out."

"You're right, you're right. Fuck!" he repeated in a whispered yell. "Everything will be okay. I covered my tracks. They won't find me. I just need to figure this out and get out of here. It's okay. Everything's okay. It's not me. They won't find me."

He kept saying they wouldn't find him, but what about *me*? Did it mean, indefinitely, that they *wouldn't* find me? Or *would* they, and if so, *how* would I be found?

This nightmare, which had started out as innocently as a man not being able to keep his eyes off of a beautiful woman, kept making it easier, and harder, to want to live. I wanted to stay alive to prove to my parents, and myself, that I could. But with them being gone, I had moments of not seeing the point. It was harder to find the will, the strength, to want to keep going. It was easier to fall victim to the circumstances I was in. To *let* myself fall. But no, I had to stop allowing myself to think that way. I just *couldn't* think, when thinking was something I'd always done best before meeting the man I didn't know I'd have to survive.

"Can we leave for Mexico now?!" I pleaded, knowing we would be spotted and stopped at the border.

"No, we have to wait. Fuck! Shut up! Let me think." At least he could.

He began to pace around the room, muttering to himself

about every detail of that night, like how he used gloves and made sure to wipe down anything he had touched.

Listening to him ramble on, having to push back the images coming to the forefront of my mind, I tried to find the answer to my question. What would happen to me?

He'd mentioned how everything pointed to me, so I couldn't help but wonder what else he could've possibly done.

"Hey, Mitch?"

"What?" he snapped.

"What did you mean by everything traced back to me?"

He turned towards me with those dark, ominous eyes, glaring at me with suspicion. I was witnessing Jason being brought to life right before my very eyes. "I took precautions," he smirked. "While you were passed out, I made sure to put your prints on the knife I used. You wouldn't want your husband to get into trouble for something like this, now, would you?!"

I found myself reverting back to the new characteristic I had picked up a few days prior. I froze, the words unable to form from my mouth. The new characteristic was unlike who I used to be.

"Would you?" he asked more aggressively.

"No." Tears forming in my eyes, blurring my vision.

"Good girl." He bent low until we were inches away from one another. His eyes still beady revealing something bad was about to come. Then in a low, hushed, husky tone he started what would become one of the most terrifying moments of my life. "Now Luke, what's the one thing you love in life more than anything else?"

I knew what he wanted me to say. And as much as I didn't want to say it, I had to. "You," I whispered.

"Right. So, we're going to play a little game. You're

going to tell me how to get into your accounts and transfer the money so I can get away. Every right answer you'll get a thrust from me." He raised his brow. "And every wrong answer . . . you'll get a little slice closer to your end."

Over the past few days, I had begun to question everything I once knew. The façade of a charmed life I lived, and this very real life experience I never thought could happen to me were now conjoining together making my own thoughts in the reality I was facing not make sense. Trying to decipher what he meant and realizing this could very well be my end, were two completely different emotions I was not ready to handle even though I had thought ending it would be easy. Knowing this could be it, made it all the more scary and all the more sad.

"What's your login?"

He grabbed me by the arm, flipping me over the side of the bed. My stomach on the mattress, feet on the ground. I stood there, bent over as he yanked my pants down and threw my laptop beside me, missing my nose by centimeters.

"What's your login?" He asked again.

"LTownsend24," I managed to get out, steadily, fully aware of what was happening to me. Throwing myself into a hollow numbness of deplete.

"Good girl."

Thrust.

My eyes closed as my teeth clenched in agonized torment.

"Password."

"RichieForever," I quivered

"I thought I was your forever?" He yanked my head back, pressing the knife hard against my neck.

"YOU ARE! YOU ARE!" I cried. "I just haven't changed it yet. I'm sorry. I'm sorry."

"Wrong." The knife started to drag slowly against the thin

skin, piercing my neck slightly. "And WHAT DO I FUCKING TELL YOU ABOUT APOLOGIZING?"

I screamed out in pain. "Capital R for Richie, capital F for forever. One word." I cried out.

Mitch started to laugh. "Well, that was a close one. I was starting to think you didn't want me inside of you anymore."

"I would never want that." I managed to say between cries.

"Okay. For that you get me again." He thrust inside of me harder than the first time. I screamed out in pain once again. "Yeah, you like that don't you?"

"Yes," I cried.

"What was that? I couldn't hear you?"

"YES."

"Good girl," he whispered. "Now what?"

My mind was empty. Left blank with fear.

"I said, what now?"

"Umm . . ." I snapped out of the trance I was in of thinking and not thinking. Trying whatever I could to not be in the reality I was in.

His question wasn't a simple one. I had no idea what to do next because I didn't handle my money. We had an accountant, well, my parents did. And when I started to make money of my own, naturally, our accountant took over the handling of my money. I only knew the login because they made me create it.

I never looked at my account because I knew I didn't need to. There would always be money there, as awful as that sounds. I was paid to live. I was given the majority of everything I owned, and when we went out, which as you know was quite often, we walked in and never saw a bill. I never thought twice about it. It became something expected because of who I was and the power I held over the people who wanted to be me.

"What's taking so long?" he growled, digging the knife further into my open wound.

"I'm thinking," I cried out. "I don't know how to transfer a large sum. I've never done it before. Try to find a number to call."

I couldn't see his face, which meant I couldn't tell what he may have been thinking. I couldn't tell if he even believed what I was saying.

"FUCK!"

Wrong answer.

"What?" I was hesitant, closing my eyes tightly afraid he was going to end it all.

"The account is flagged. Shit!"

"Why would it be flagged?" The heaviness of his body weight fell on me as he hunched over to look closely at the screen.

"Because they're looking for us, Luke. They don't want us leaving the fucking country. God, for someone so beautiful, you're dumb as shit. They can probably track us here. FUCK!"

"It's okay Mitch. Let's just calm down and think for a minute. We'll figure it out."

By that point he had gotten off of me and began to pace the room wielding the knife in a crazed manner. He was unreadable. Unpredictable.

I sat up, reaching to catch the blood running down my neck, thankful I was still alive. "Maybe if we just start driving up north to Canada, they won't be able to track us."

"Why would we do that when we could just cross here and disappear?"

"You're right. You're right. That's a better idea. A smarter idea." Every ounce of my being hated how I had to go along with what he was saying. I not only had to think about myself and getting help, or found, but I had to take my captor's feelings into consideration. My captor, who foolishly convinced me to become his wife when I was in a tough place, mentally. This had been the most unbelievable week, full of the maximum heartache, pain, and terror anyone could handle, but the most unbelievable part was how I had not seen *any* of this coming. Everyone else could, in a way. And they were right. But *why* were they all right? And why wasn't I able to see it? Or at least why didn't I listen when they were telling me these things? Or try to find proof for myself?

"Sit against the headboard."

"Why?" I asked.

"Shut up! Stop asking so many fucking questions." He was annoyed, and I kept making it worse.

I got quiet and did what he told me to do. He then tied my other hand to the one that was already tied to the dresser. Mitch's next move was to put tape over my mouth and tie my ankles together, making it impossible to escape.

My perception of time over the course of the week had been moving indifferently for me. Lying there, missing my parents, missing my friends, missing the life I lived and took for granted, before this nightmare, had me feeling angry at myself for living so carelessly. Living each day so selfishly and not utilizing the privilege I had to do something greater. I stayed tied like that until I eventually fell asleep.

I don't know how long it was between the time I drifted off to sleep and when I was startled awake to pounding on the door. Fear and panic quickly flooded me as I scrambled to sit up, not knowing what or who was on the other side. The pounding grew heavier, vibrating the wall behind me.

BAM! BAM! BAM!

Until the door was busted down and a swarm of armed FBI agents made their way into the small room surrounding the bed.

I started to scream, "It was Mitch! It was Mitch!" as soon as the tape was ripped from my mouth.

"Luke Townsend, you are under arrest for the murder of Orson and Carter Townsend. You have the right to remain silent . . ."

"What? What are you talking about? I didn't kill my parents. Please! Help me!"

Everything happened so quickly. I was cut from the bed ties, rushed outside with my hands cuffed behind my back and in all of the commotion I didn't even notice Mitch was nowhere in sight. I did, however, see the little girl from earlier being held tightly in her mother's arms. The two of them stared at me, the little girl looking frightened.

I tried, once again, through my eyes, to convey that everything was okay. Everything *would* be okay. Her mother pulled her into her body, cradling her head against her shoulder, hugging her even tighter than before, to protect her just like a mother would do to her child.

"What are you guys doing? Why am I being arrested?" I asked the agents when they got into the car. "Where's Mitch? Or Jason, or whatever his name is? He did it! Did you catch him?"

I didn't get any answers. They were silent the entire drive to the police station. As I sat there feeling relieved, scared, and not knowing what I was about to be thrown into, I reminded myself that it couldn't be any worse than what I'd already endured.

Even if I was going to jail, I had been saved.

Chapter Sixteen

Once we arrived at the police station, I was quickly ushered into an interrogation room where the handcuffs were taken off of me. When I looked up with relief, I realized I wasn't alone. I was met with a room full of people seemingly happy I was there, safe.

"Ms. Townsend, we're sorry we had to bring you in this way. We want to let you know that we're glad you're safe."

"What's going on? Did you find him? It was Mitch, or Jason, whatever his name is. He did it. He killed my parents. I didn't do it. Please! You have to believe me," I spewed, trying to plea my innocence.

"We know, Ms. Townsend," he paused. "Let me introduce myself, I'm special agent Kai with the FBI and this is my partner special agent Whitmore. We've known it was Mr. Feldstein since we were first contacted by the Beverly Hills P.D." He spoke so eloquently with a calmness behind his tone, reassuring me, a victim, how everything would be alright. "We've actually been looking for Mr. Feldstein, or as you know him, Mr. Bellamy, for quite some time pertaining to some criminal activity he's done in the past." Agent Kai looked at me remorsefully. "He's a wanted man, Ms. Townsend. We're just sorry that it had to come down to this; you being a part of it and," he cleared his throat, "Losing your parents. For that, you have our deepest condolences. We hope to give you peace of mind that we're going to get him."

"What is he wanted for?" I asked, tensely, only now realizing we, especially me, were all in over our heads when it came to Mitch Bellamy. He had been a handsome stranger who won me over. A normal, foolish young woman who let him into my life all out of curiosity and a feeling of being desired. It just showed how clever he was to be able to get away from the FBI and to be wanted by them. If they couldn't catch him the first time, how did they expect to catch him now?

"Well, Ma'am . . ."

"Please. Call me Luke."

"Yes, Ms. Townsend," Special Agent Whitmore said. "Mr. Feldstein has a criminal past. I'm not sure if he ever revealed any of that information to you." I shrugged, slightly. "But he's been in and out of jail since he was a minor. There's a lot of petty theft in his record, but he was also let off on a mistrial for committing two murders, prior to your parents'." He looked at me sympathetically. "Once again, we're so sorry for your loss, but this is why we're looking for him now. We have new evidence connecting him to a few other murders and are now sure it was him for the two that were a mistrial."

"What?" My heart fell to the pit of my stomach. "Yeah, he mentioned something about murdering two girls but I . . . I . . . I think I might be sick." I took a few deep breaths. "How did he . . . what do you mean, mur . . . I'm sorry, I . . ."

"It's okay, Ms. Townsend, we understand this is hard to hear. We can give you a minute."

"No." I shook off. "Keep going."

"Mr. Feldstein murdered two young women in Ohio about three years ago, where he got off on a mistrial followed by an acquittal. The jury couldn't come to an agreement on whether or not the evidence proved he, in fact, actually committed the murders or if it was a mistake."

"A mistake? How do you accidentally *murder* someone?" Baffled by the word, I sat there, panic washing over me in waves knowing I was with a murderer. All of a sudden, it was like him killing my parents directly in front of me was somehow just now becoming something that actually happened instead of something I was hoping I made up. The state of shock I had been in—the survival mode, if you will—had instantly worn off, and I could now see what was really in front of me: a killer.

"There's a sexual fetish some people are into," agent Kai began, "Where the woman gets into a bath of ice water for twenty minutes and then their partner takes them out of the water and has sex with them and in a way . . . brings them back to life."

I shook my head, frivolously, feeling like this was all too much. "What does that have to do with any of this?"

"Well, that's where he got off on the mistrial. The jury couldn't decide if he was pursuing a sexual fetish and was a little too late in retrieving each victim out of the water, or if he was actively trying to kill them. In which he proceeded to have sex with their dead bodies."

"Okay, now I'm really going to be sick." I leaned over just as special agent Whitmore slid the trashcan next to me.

After vomiting, I sat up and was offered some water, but all I could do was cry, feeling like I had been violated in more ways than one.

"After he was let off, he robbed a bank and would've gotten away with it, but he chose to violate his parole by fleeing the state of Ohio. A few months back, we got word of a few more of these types of murders happening in and around the state of Ohio and every scene was left the same. We're lead to believe that it was Mr. Feldstein." Agent Whitmore looked to Agent Kai.

"Which is where *you* come into all of this, Ms. Townsend. Mr. Feldstein changed his identity and began to pursue you. We don't know every detail as to how or what he did exactly, but we were filled in during a phone conversation between the police and a private investigator your parents hired on our drive here. Since he's on our wanted list, we were notified by the Beverly Hills PD."

Over the course of a few hours, I told them the story of what happened. *Everything* that happened. Starting from the moment I first caught him staring at me to how he murdered my parents, proceeded to kidnap me, rape me, and how we ended up at the motel where they found me. It was hard having to relive it. The hardest part being recounting what happened to my parents and seeing their faces so vividly in my mind, giving me their last looks.

The agents assured me they would get him. They promised. I knew promises could be broken, though; Richie broke the first one ever made to me. But there I was having to trust a group of people I didn't know. Although they were the FBI, still, it wasn't so easy for me to do anymore. I had to have faith in them that they would do the job they were trained to do.

To get him.

"Can I ask you something?"

"You can ask us anything, Ms. Townsend."

"How did you find me? I mean, how did you know I was at the motel?"

"We received two calls with sightings of you there. The

first was from a woman saying her daughter recognized you as the woman in the car when they turned on the television. The second was an anonymous tip from a caller who we believe to have been Mr. Feldstein himself, in an attempt to distract us so he could get away." Agent Kai paused. "But we know it wasn't you, Ms. Townsend. We want to emphasize that because even though he tried to set you up, we've known Mr. Feldstein was up to something for quite some time. We were anticipating it. We just didn't know what it would be and now we'd like your help."

"Help?" I questioned. "How can *I* help? I mean, I'll do anything to get him but isn't it your . . . I mean, I . . . Help?!"

"This is where it's going to be a little bit hard."

"What do you mean by that? How could things be any harder than they've already have?"

"We want you to work with us, Ms. Townsend. Basically, you'd be undercover."

"What?!"

"We would like you to keep up this act of being guilty. That's why we went in as aggressively as we did to retrieve you. Our plan is to release it to the media, which is where that hard part comes in, because it might be hard on you." He paused before continuing bluntly. "People are going to rip you apart. They're going to say you murdered your parents for money. You'll find out just how cruel people can really be. It's not going to be easy, Ms. Townsend."

I looked up with hesitation in my eyes. They knew what they were asking of me. I could hear it in their voices. They were asking me to give up the entire life I once knew. Not that I assumed everything would magically go back to normal, I knew it wouldn't. My life would never be the same again. *I* would ever be the same again.

My life would be torn apart scaling the entire world. I

would no longer be the socialite on the cover of every tabloid. I wouldn't be the coveted 'muse' for designers or artists my parents were friends with. I wouldn't be the girl everyone modeled their lives after; the girl everyone wanted to become. I would now be the most hated, most misunderstood person in the world. The most judged.

Even if the FBI *could* fix everything in the end by putting a statement out about the elaborate "task force" that went into catching someone on their most wanted list, I would be known as the woman, the girl, who fell in love with a cold-hearted killer. As much as I didn't want to be that person, that unrecognizable shell of a woman, I *was* her. I *was* that person, even if I lied to myself that I wasn't. I still was and would *always* be. If you're looking at it from an insider's perspective, all of that wouldn't matter because I had to do whatever I could to get justice for my parents. My beloved parents. It was my fault they were now dead and there would be no amount of retribution against me that would ever change that. I would be blamed for it all, for the rest of my life, by *everyone*. But mostly by *me*.

"Okay. I'll do it."

"Are you sure, Ms. Townsend? You do understand the lengths we're asking you to go through, right?"

"I do." I nodded, tears forming in the corners of my eyes. "It's the least I can do for my parents after . . . *everything* they did for me."

There was a saddened silence that filled the room for a few minutes before being broken by agent Kai. "Okay, now, Ms. Townsend, we're going to escort you back to Los Angeles. You'll be staying in the jail, but in an interrogation room. It's for your own protection, and will only be for about a day until we make it seem as if you've posted bail. We are currently alerting the media about you being transferred. We will alert them again when you've posted bail." He sat down on the edge of the table and loosened his otherwise impeccable posture. "We're going to have undercover police officers escorting you and staying with you the entire time for your safety. So, if you need *anything* please let one of them know. They're going to appear to be friends or family. When you are being escorted out of the car at your home please act as if you know them. The media *will* be there, taking videos and photographs as this is a high-profile case. We want that. We want Mr. Feldstein to see that."

"Okay."

"This is where a very key element is going to come into play for us." Agent Whitmore took over the conversation. "Our *hope,* is that Mr. Feldstein will try to get in contact with you. He'll more than likely know we have the phones tapped. So, we're hoping that if *you* can think of any way to get a hold of him, you can. Or we're hoping he'll somehow come to see you or get in touch with you in some way. Once he does, you need to continue to act as if *we're* the bad guys and he is right. It's a psychological thing with men like him. He needs to feel in control, like he can trust you. He needs to feel like you *need* him. Like you need *his* help. Will you be able to do that?"

I hung my head low. "Yes, I will."

"Okay. Good, Ms. Townsend, but . . . ." he lingered. "Here's another part which may or may not be hard for you, given everything you've already been through."

I looked up to meet Agent Whitmore's serious expression.

"If he asks, we want you to leave with him."

"What?" Panic came over me again as I looked between the two agents with concern.

"We know it sounds overwhelming, especially because you were just with Mr. Feldstein, but we feel this is our best chance at getting him. We normally wouldn't ask something like this of you, but, like I said, this is considered a high-profile case and we need to take action as soon as possible." Agent Whitmore looked for my reaction. "We'll have a tracking device in the button of your jeans, and you're going to have to wear a wire."

Agent Kai took over. "We want you to essentially be alone with Mr. Feldstein to illicit a confession of the murder of your parents and whatever other details you can get from him for the previous murders of the two women and possibly the others we believe him to be connected to."

My bottom lip began to quiver as the tears began to fall more rapidly down my cheeks. "I . . ." I couldn't speak. I was at a loss for words. Even if I did have them, I don't think the words would've been able to come out. They were . . . frozen.

"Ms. Townsend," Agent Whitmore began the conversation again. "We understand this is asking more of you than we may have initially eluded to, but this is a plan we think will work. And we'll have a team following you the entire time, who will be able to take him out at any sign of a struggle. We can *guarantee* that to you, Ms. Townsend. Nothing bad will happen to you. We won't let it."

I shook my head yes without giving it another thought. I was going to do it. Not for me; for my parents. Sometimes, what you think may be your greatest creation, could be your biggest work of destruction. That's what I now was to them. I was their failed masterpiece. Their one work of art no one would love forever. I had already been paying for it, why not let it continue a little while longer while I was mentally still in it.

"Where are my parents now?" I asked when I was finally able to speak. "And how did they . . ."

"They're in the umm . . ." He cleared his throat. "Your

parents are in the morgue, Ms. Townsend. We have the coroner doing their autopsies now. But umm, they were left there for days. And umm . . . well, upon further investigation, the heater was set to a high temperature. So, when they were discovered . . . they were in pretty bad shape. They, umm . . ." It was hard for him to get the words out. His stoic demeanor had fallen. He did have some empathy in him after all.

I started to cry. Everything was my fault. *Everything*. If I would've known all of this was going to happen, especially to my parents, then I wouldn't have . . . I should've just . . . stayed living the way I was. Masking the heartache I was in with an illusion of a girl who had it all; the fame, the fortune, the partying, and the men I had in secret. Which wasn't a bad way to live. It just didn't have what my heart desired and I let my heart speak over my head in a time where I was at my lowest and no one, not even myself, knew it.

"We have some people here who might be of some comfort to you." Agent Whitmore motioned to the guard who then opened the door and in walked Remy, Franklin, and Margot.

Seeing them and feeling the warmth, the familiarity, the love they brought in, made me break down in their embraces. "Luke, we're so sorry. We're so, so sorry. We should've done more. We should've told you about him when your Mom told us about who he really was." Remy gently stroked my back.

I should've been angry. I should've yelled. I should've screamed. I should've punched each one of them in the face.

How could they not tell me? I had very few people in my life whom I trusted wholeheartedly. My parents and my three friends. Everyone else only used me to try and get some sort of fame or notoriety. But them. My people. Internally I was in a fit of rage with how everything that transpired could have been avoided. I could easily blame them, the three before me, my best friends. But if I got mad at them, then I would really have no one left. And even if they did tell me, what happened still could have happened. No one knew. How could they?

With all of the information that had just been presented to me, I could have fallen to the floor kicking and screaming, throwing a tantrum which would have been well accounted for. I just didn't have it in me.

So, I didn't get mad. I just leaned into the comfort of the people who loved me.

"Yeah Luke, we're here for you, *always*. We love you," Margot said.

"We're going to get through this. We promise," Franklin added.

"But do you . . . do you know what I have to do?" I whispered.

"Yeah, we know, but we know you can do it. You're Luke Fucking Townsend. Besides, you've got us Luke. You've always got us." Remy hugged me tighter.

I sat there quietly, unsure if I should be thankful the people I loved most in the world would be there for me when they could have been there for me already. Ultimately, thinking about everything I went through, it was a nice feeling to have when what I had experienced left me empty and numb.

"How did you get here so fast?"

Margot smiled. "We took a helicopter."

"Nothing would *ever* stop us from being here, Luke. Even if we couldn't see you, we'd still be here," Franklin reassured.

"Okay, Ms. Townsend," Agent Kai began, "Are you ready? We're going to start this now."

I looked at each one of my friends almost as if I were looking at them for the last time because in a way it was. No one knew the outcome of what was about to happen. Mitch had disappeared and there was no telling if he would return. But if he did, and I did make it out, I wouldn't be the Luke my friends once knew. I would be someone *I* didn't even know. I would be reinvented, not by my own choosing.

I gave them each a hug. "Yeah," I nodded, holding back more tears. "I guess so."

Agent Kai then placed handcuffs on me before proceeding to walk me, along with Agent Whitmore, out through the back of the precinct to an armored van waiting for us. There were cameras flashing, reporters screaming my name, bystanders asking me why I did it. They were yelling I was evil, asking how I could kill my own parents. They didn't know this wasn't real. *I* knew this wasn't real. I'd been warned this was going to happen. So, when it actually was, the emotional toll it took on me for those 10 seconds of walking from the door and into the van hurt me to my core. It's a feeling I'll never forget. Because in that moment, I felt like I did truly do it. Not him. Not anyone. Just me.

Chapter Seventeen

My time in the interrogation room was as promised, short. I was out within a day. Even though I was alone in my own space, I was still terrified. Being in jail is not somewhere people usually see themselves going to. Especially when they didn't even do what they were put in there for. You hear about that sometimes. People being wrongly convicted of a crime. It was no different for me, I was put in there to play a part for the media which was something I'd always done. But this time it was for *him*. So, even though being in there wasn't technically real, I was still in there. It was real. I was experiencing it.

When I was released, the amount of reporters and bystanders lining the street was chaotic. I knew they were there to blame me or to say they were there on their social media platforms to say they were a part of it in some way. Ignoring the screams was all I could do. I kept repeating to myself that these people were there because they loved my parents.

As we turned onto the familiar road, everything had now become dim as the nightmare of that night replayed in the back of my mind like a movie continuously playing on a loop. I wasn't just going back to my family home, *my* home, I was going back to the scene of the crime. A place once filled with so much light and happiness. A place that was a part of me, but that part, along with this place, had now faded to a darkness I could only hope to forget, but knew I never could.

My nerves were rattling inside of me as we got closer and I could hear them before I could see them. Strangers, familiar faces and reporters lined the streets all there to shun the girl they once revered as untouchable. 'Murderers aren't welcome,' 'Selfish Bitch,' and 'Money Hungry Whore' were just a few of the signs being held by these people. If I'm being honest, if I were in their shoes I'd probably think the same thing.

Janelle, one of the undercover agents escorting me, took my hand and squeezed it reassuring me everything would be okay. In my heart, I knew none of this would ever be okay though. The hope I was holding on to of one day starting a new life away from this one, was completely lost to all of the chaos surrounding me now.

Once we were inside of the property and the gates closed, I felt a little more at ease knowing no one would be able to see me. I was used to being seen, but now all I wanted to do was disappear. Although the yelling from the other side of the gate was still loud, not being able to be seen made it easier.

"Let's get inside," Janelle suggested.

Inside. Where my personal space kept me completely hidden from the world, except it was no longer a place of sanctuary. It had become a place invaded by a handful of FBI agents there to watch me round the clock.

I looked at her in agreement.

I will admit, it was nice having another woman with me. I know she didn't know exactly what I was going through, or maybe she did in her line of work, but it was nice to have someone who could kind of *get* how I was feeling, or at least seem to. Of course, I had low moments, thinking she was judging me. She was this beautiful, strong woman who seemed to be able to take care of herself. To compare us to one another, she was an FBI agent, and I was a woman who never wanted for anything, who let someone into my life who ended up manipulating me. Which ultimately lead me to pay for it by my parents being murdered. She didn't come off as a person who would ever let something like that happen to her. She was strong and I was weak. She could stand up for herself and I couldn't, even though at one point in my life, that's what I thought I was doing.

The officers who surrounded me made a barrier from the outside world, protecting me as we began the walk towards the pool house. My breathing grew rapid as flashes of that night began playing in the forefront of my mind. Reliving it and all of the emotions which came along with what I'd experienced, created an overwhelming feeling of sadness. I stared at my feet to keep my focus centered, but I knew I would have to eventually look up. I *had* to look at my parents' house. I had to look at the room it happened in because even though I knew it was real, it still felt like I was living in a dream. If I didn't look then, I'd always be waiting to hear my mother's voice calling from the patio.

The curtains were drawn open and the little breath I was holding in started to come out slowly. I stopped walking, gazing at the room from a new perspective. It looked different. The house that allowed me to live a "normal" life had now lost the life I always thought it had. It lost everything I loved about it. The people I loved about it. As if it were more important than anything else happening in my life, I became panicked remembering a detail which made absolutely no sense for the moment of reflection I was in.

He had changed the locks to the pool house, and we wouldn't be able to get in. "I don't know the code."

"What code?" Janelle looked confused.

"For the door. Mi . . . he changed the locks to the kind where you need a code. I don't know it. We can't get in. How do we . . . "

"It's okay Luke, we've taken care of everything. You don't have to worry about that," one of the male agents reassured from behind me.

It was easier said than done. My head started spinning, my chest felt tight, my breathing quickened, and my heart began to race. I managed to get to the door, but once it was opened and I walked inside, the memory of those days of being locked in there with him came rushing back and I fell to the floor with a scream. It was all too much trying to hold every anxiety ridden feeling in, but having it all release made it feel a little bit better.

"Breathe, Luke. Just breathe. It's okay." I heard a voice, but couldn't tell who it was coming from. The room felt like it was spinning. "I think you might be having an anxiety attack. It's completely normal," the voice reassured. "Just take some deep breaths with me. Inhale . . . and exhale. There you go."

I began to calm down.

This wasn't normal though, not normal by any means. I had the weight of the world on my shoulders because I was being blamed for murdering the world's beloved Orson and

Carter Townsend, *my parents*. How could anybody do such a thing? I could make myself appear to be calmed down, but inside, I never would be.

The agents managed to get me on the couch where I lied down and was able to catch my breath. "I don't know what I'm supposed to do now," I wept. "How am I supposed to get in contact with him? I don't even know who he really is. I only know the made-up version he was to me. I, I . . . I don't know if I can do this." I looked to the ceiling, my bottom lip quivering as my eyes filled to a blur.

"You can Luke. We all know you can." Janelle put her hand on mine as she knelt down beside me. "Listen, I know it's tough, but everyone in this room and everyone on this case knows *you* didn't do anything wrong. We know you didn't kill your parents. We know you're a good person." She was trying to be as sincere as she could, but she didn't know the excruciating amount of guilt I felt. No one did. "We're here to help you help the FBI get this guy so you can get back to your regular life."

"I don't think that's ever going to happen."

"It can. And if you want it enough, it will. I mean, it won't be exactly the same, but you'll be liked again. People will commend you for doing this for your parents," she smiled.

"Is that what you think of me?" I turned to meet her gaze. "That I only care about people liking me?"

"No. I just know you would probably prefer everything be how it *was*, instead of living in whatever we would call this now. Fear? Denial?"

"That's a bold assumption. You don't even know me."

She never faltered with her response. She was trained to not show emotion or empathy for me. She just continued to *be*. "It'll take time, and maybe some therapy, but the truth *will* come out for you. Eventually, people will forget about hating you for a little while, and remember why they've always loved you. Why they've always loved your parents," she paused. "People make mistakes, Luke, everyone knows that. If you feel like people won't understand, just know that this will humanize you to them. I mean, seeing someone you regard as being up on a pedestal their whole life, falling just as hard as you can, makes the world seem not as big as it appears. When the time comes, when this is all over, it'll all be okay. *You'll* be okay. That's the only thing that matters."

Sleep had left me again. I had strangers in my home, and I was in very close proximity to where my parents were murdered right in front of me, which was *still* the only image I could see every time I closed my eyes. I would shake my head trying to clear my thoughts, but they always went back to them, to that night. On the off chance I wasn't thinking about that night, my thoughts were in a race with themselves circling around, trying to remember every word Mitch had ever said to me to try and find some sort of clue on how I could get in touch with him.

I couldn't think of a way though. He was a ghost to me. He disappeared just as quickly as he first made himself known. Those revolving thoughts were unsettling, and I knew I needed something to make me feel comforted.

I got out of bed, making my way to the closet where I kept my safe. I wanted to make sure my most prized possessions, jewelry my mother had given me, were still in there where I kept them safe and tucked away from the world. They were too precious and sentimental to share with anyone. They were mine and now the only things I had left of my mother. Those are what I wanted to grab before we fled that day, but he wouldn't let me take them. The sad realization of how they could have been taken away from me forever hung in the back of my mind.

I was just about to turn the handle when I remembered he'd changed the code on the safe as well. My heart sank, but something still wanted me to try. I *had* to.

My hand reached out, gripping the handle tightly, every part of me shaking from the nerves welling up inside.

And just like that, joy flooded back to my heart when I turned the handle and it broke off. Obviously, the FBI needed to cover every inch of their case so they had to do what they could to get it open. The sinking feeling returned, thinking about how even more of my life had been invaded.

I reached inside of my safe, feeling around for the felt pouch my treasures were zipped inside of. I could feel the cold, bare touch of the metal on my palm and the sinking of my heart to the pit of my stomach.

"No, no, no. It has to be here. It has to! Please, Mom! Please let it be here."

Relief fell upon me as my fingertips felt the soft, familiar feeling of everything I had left. I pulled the pouch out, bringing it to my chest, crying tears of joy mixed with heartache. I missed my mother. I didn't know how I could go on without her. I didn't think I could be strong like her. I began talking to her silently, in my head. I responded to myself, as if she were there comforting me, telling me she was okay and that everything would come to light.

Just then I heard a creak in the floorboards. My heart dropped. It was him. He'd come to kill me.

"They made sure only to take what they could use as evidence."

I let out the breath I didn't realize I was holding.

My pulse slowed. I gave a faint smile, hoping it would suffice her concern and she would leave me alone. She didn't take the hint and sat down next to me instead.

"I wanted to apologize to you Luke, for earlier. I didn't mean to hurt your feelings and I can only *imagine* what you're going through. I didn't mean anything by it. I was just . . . trying to let you know that everything *can* be okay again, even if it takes a while."

"Thanks," I said, not taking my eyes from inside the bag.

"You know, your parents would be proud of you. I mean, I know I didn't know them, but I've always been a fan of theirs, and of *yours*," she smirked. "They loved you. They still do. They always will, even if they aren't here."

The empathy I thought was trained out of her was still there. After all, she was still human. I appreciated how she was being nice to me, but I still felt like I couldn't do anything to help the situation I was in.

"I don't know how to contact him." I looked to her. "And I don't know if I even want to because it means I'll have to see him. And he . . . hurt me."

"What if we try and make a game out of it?" she suggested.

"What do you mean?"

"Well, let's look for clues around here. I'm sure something was overlooked. I mean, you *know* him, or the version of him you know, better than any FBI agent. No matter how much they think they know their case, something can always be overlooked. Then when it comes time to talk to him and see him, you just pretend like he's the incredible man you fell head over heels in love with. I know it sounds scary, but we'll take it one step at a time," she paused. "Try to forget what you now know about him and pretend that you still care about him. Just for a short little while, try to trick your brain. Then we'll come in and take him from you. *I promise.* We won't let anything happen to you, Luke. He can't hurt you anymore. All of that's done, we've got you." She reached down and squeezed my hand.

I was putting my life back in the hands of someone I didn't know, granted, this time around it was the FBI, but still, I was scared.

Since I couldn't sleep, we started to play the game. I started to look around the pool house, starting with the safe, to see if there was anything Mitch may have left behind. I did that for days, looking for anything out of the ordinary, waiting to see if somehow, he would try to contact me. It was almost like a fun distraction to keep my mind off of the pain of losing my parents. The strange thing though was that I didn't go outside. I wouldn't allow it. I kept myself trapped in my own nightmare, since anything I needed was brought to me, making it easier to hide. That's all I wanted to do. However, I did leave all of the windows and doors open to feel like I could get out if I wanted. Knowing I could made me less nervous.

The only curtains I kept closed were the ones facing my parents' house. The ones facing that room. I couldn't bear to look at the windows where they were slain on the other side. It made me cry to even think that that *spot* was so close to where I was. It was no longer just a room in the house. It was a room that held the worst memory of my entire life.

Chapter Eighteen

Days passed before we regrouped with Agents Kai and Whitmore to see if they had any Intel on Mitch's whereabouts. There was no trace of him, he had completely vanished. However, my face was still plastered all over the news with made up stories of how I killed my parents. Some media outlets reported I did it because they hated the man I married. Some reported I killed them for their money. Having my name slandered, in such a public way, made me feel deeply depressed with how much hatred and blatant lies were being said about me. My reputation that I had worked so hard to build, whether you may have liked it or not, was now tarnished in a way I felt I could never come back from. I knew it didn't matter, and I didn't really care, but in those brief moments where I would catch a glimpse of what the world was saying, I would fall deeper into that depression where I felt like I was the loneliest person in the world.

It must have been boring for the agents protecting me to be sitting around in silence all day, but, every time one of them tried to turn on the TV I would jump up and tell them no. I was trapped and couldn't even watch a program without my name and the horrors of who I was to the world, plastered on the screens for everyone to see and judge.

The world and the FBI had me locked inside of our property, but I had myself locked inside of the pool house. I could technically walk around the grounds, but it was hard. Everything reminded me of my parents. So, once again, I was a prisoner in my own home.

Janelle finally talked me into getting some fresh air after seeing how apprehensive and on edge I was. "It'll be good for you."

Taking that first step across the threshold was the hardest. When I hesitated, Janelle shielded me from the view of the last memory of my parents. She walked with me to the tennis court and said I should take some time for myself and let the sun hit my skin before turning to go back to the pool house, leaving me in whatever serenity I could find.

Without realizing it, I began to walk the path Mitch and I had walked to escape that day. All I could think about was how I missed what everyone else was seeing in him that I couldn't. He was handsome, charming, loving, endearing even. He seemed to truly care about me, until he didn't. It was obvious how I could easily fall in love with him as hard as I did. He was what I didn't know I needed. A kind, good-looking, smart man who could take care of me. What I couldn't see was what made everyone question him and our relationship. The lie, the act he was putting on, I couldn't see it. To me he was a gentleman who loved me in a way I'd never been loved before.

He was different from Richie. Although I was in love with both, Richie brought me to sadness and Mitch brought me back to life. Lost in these thoughts of finding love again after grief put me at ease and gave me the strength to feel like I *could* do this. I *could* face him if it came to that. Deep down, as much as I was terrified, I was hoping it would for my parents' sake.

Walking along the walkway, I couldn't help but get lost in my own thoughts. I may as well have been somewhere else. I know I wished I was. The fresh air hitting my face and filling my lungs helped me to finally be able to relax from everything that was going on. I was one with the Los Angeles nature, breathing in slowly, trying to come to terms with how I would continue living without my parents. What would I even do? Where would I even live? Nothing seemed important and no one would probably even care what happened to me after all of this.

I was breathing out the anxiety I was holding in when the snap of a twig from the hedges beside me startled me back to reality. I glanced around surveying the grounds, but nothing.

Just as my heart began to steady from the rush of fear that was riddling my body, I felt the all too familiar feeling of being watched.

I looked to the pool house but didn't see any of my protectors in sight. My body lost all control and began to shake as the suspicion of not being alone arose within me.

I slowly turned in the direction I felt it coming from. My breath was taken away from me as I saw the eyes that started it all. Peering at me through the hedges was this stranger, this murderer, this someone I called my husband.

He motioned for me to come closer. I stood still, terrified. The breath that had escaped me came back slowly as I cautiously inched my way over.

"They think it's you. That's good. That's what I wanted."

The sound of his voice ignited a fire inside of me. I had to see him pay for what he had done to my family, to *me*. Any apprehension I had been going back and forth with left and I knew the role I had to play in catching this man I had grown to hate.

I looked towards the pool house to make sure no one was watching me and ran to be closer to him. "Mitch, I've missed you. Why didn't you take me with you?"

He narrowed his expression.

"Mitch, let me come with you. Please!" I pleaded. "We can run away. Far away this time, where no one will find us. I'm on your side, Mitch. I've always been on your side. You know that." I heard a noise coming from the direction of the pool house and turned to see if anyone was coming. "I don't think I have much time. They're always watching me, waiting for me to mess up. They want me in prison for this. You did a good job, they don't think it was you at all," I paused, eager to get things going so it could all be over. "I love you. I love you so much, Mitch. Please take me with you! You're the only one I want to be with. You're the only one I have left. You're my, everything. You're my home. My *husband*." I looked into his dark, dead eyes and could feel a chill running down my spine. There was a darkness within him I couldn't see, the evil, until that very moment.

"Okay," he finally answered. "Meet me here at 10 o'clock tonight. I know they leave around 9:30. That'll give you some time in case they come back for something."

He'd been watching, just like Agents Kai and Whitmore said he would if he were to return. We had an entire decoy of agents who would arrive at seven o'clock in the morning and leave at 9:30 p.m. each night. Both teams each had identical agent counterparts with similar build, hair color and style. They also all wore hats and sunglasses when leaving and entering the property, so it always appeared like the same set of agents were coming and going when really, there was a set of agents who stayed with me 24/7.

The intention of the decoy agents was to make Mitch think I was alone at night in the hopes he would see an open opportunity to come onto the property as I would be alone.

"Yes. I can and I *will* baby. I'll do anything to be with you."

"Don't bring anything. Don't make it obvious," he began to say. "Meet me in this exact spot. I'll have a car waiting and we'll get you out of here. We'll get out of here together."

I smiled, trying to go in for a kiss I didn't want to give. Thankfully, he pulled back. "They could be watching. I don't want them to see me."

"You're right. You're *always* right." It pained me to say that. "I'll be here at 10. I can't wait to be safe in your arms already. Can't you take me now?"

"No, they would catch us. It has to be tonight after they leave."

"Okay, Mitch. I trust you." My head jolted to my left as I heard footsteps approaching. "Someone's coming." I turned to say to him, but he had already gone.

"Hey Luke, is everything okay?" Janelle called.

"Oh yeah, I was just looking at this hedge. I thought I saw an injured bird in here. I must be losing my mind," I said hoping he would hear the lie I was making for him. Hoping he could feel like he could trust me even though it was hard to pretend to do that. Inside, there was this delusional sense that I still felt something for him, even after everything he did. I was heartbroken for losing another person I loved.

"Let's get back inside."

"Okay. Good idea," I answered. The anticipation of spilling every detail of the conversation I had just had couldn't make my legs walk fast enough.

～

"Are you serious?" One of the agents asked, seeming shocked and ready for action as he jumped out of his chair, reaching for the gun in his holster.

"We should've had someone close by," another one said.

"No," I answered. "I played my part. He's going to come get me tonight. I'm meeting him out back in the same spot and none of you can be anywhere in sight." I looked at everyone individually. "This was the plan, right? To go with him and get the confession?" I nodded. "It's happening tonight. Let Agents Kai and Whitmore know and set me up with whatever you need to. I'm ready to do this. I'm not scared shitless anymore. I just want to get him." I emphasized, smacking my hands to my knees.

"Since when did you become one of us?" an agent joked.

"Luke." Janelle stood up to hug me. "You did good. We're gonna get him."

"Yeah. We are."

I couldn't eat. I couldn't rest at all. I was anxious and nervous for the time to come already. I still had an entire day to wait out. In a way it was good to have that time even though I wanted it to go by as fast as it could because it gave us time to think of possible ways to bring up what happened. We discussed trigger words that could set him off. We discussed things I should definitely *not* say no matter how bad I wanted to. For a while the agents even taught me ways to defend myself if it came down to it. I was ready. Well, as ready as I ever would be.

"Listen, you've got this Luke. We have cars stashed around the neighborhood that we're going to jump into and follow at distance. Remember, you have the tracker in the button of your jeans. For the wire, don't even worry about shuffling around because we'll be able to hear you just fine. Just try to not let him umm," Janelle paused. "Try not to let him take your shirt off. I know you're playing this part, but you don't have to do anything you don't want to do or don't feel comfortable with. Okay?"

"Yeah, I got it. Trust me. I got it." I nodded.

This was it. This was the moment my life would finally mean something. The moment I was going to him *no matter what it took.*

Chapter Nineteen

I went out a few minutes before I had to be there. I tried to make it appear as if I were "sneaking out," just in case he was watching me. I even looked over my shoulder a few times, ducking down to hide as if I thought I'd heard something. Making it believable for him wasn't hard to do because I needed to look scared, and I was. There was no hiding that. I was willingly putting myself in a dangerous position, leaving with a murderer, my husband, where the outcome was uncertain. Yes, I had the peace of mind that the FBI would step in at a moment's notice, but there was no telling what Mitch, Jason, would do. After all, he already fooled me once into loving him and I wasn't going to let him fool me again.

When I got to the spot by the hedges, I waited patiently wondering if he was actually going to show up. I began to look around the property, trying to see if maybe he was going to come at me from a different angle wielding the knife he loved so much. But I was stopped dead in my scanning.

My family home was lit up, looking so regal. I never paid much attention to the detailing of the architecture my parents loved about our home. For example, they would question the architect's reasoning for placing a certain window in the corner. Little things like that no one else would ever think of.

But there she was, the lights shining upon her making her seem like the greatest creation ever made. There was so much beauty on her outside that you'd never be able to tell the pain and sadness she held on the inside.

Minutes past before I finally heard some shuffling nearby. I looked cautiously only to be met by a hand popping out motioning me to come over.

Taking a deep breath to control my racing heart, I took the first step towards justice.

"I thought you weren't going to come." I fell into him, embracing him in a tight hug.

"I was watching to make sure you weren't being followed," he responded.

I hugged him tighter, hoping to show how I thought he was a good "protector."

"I love you, Mitch," I whispered.

"Good. Now stop talking and follow me." He reached for my arm and started to pull me through the hedges, each branch scraping my bare arms every step of the way.

When we got to the street, we briskly walked to a dark van parked halfway down the block. The engine was still running. "Get in the back. I'll tell you when it's safe to come up front."

"Should I cover up? Or are you going to tie me to something?"

"Do I need to?"

Panic came over me, thinking I may have outed myself in some way. "No, I just didn't know if you wanted to. I just want to get out of here and start our lives together already."

"Okay, well get the fuck in the van." He shoved me in and slammed the door shut.

I could barely see inside, but the smell of bleach was prominent. Something had definitely happened in there and I really didn't want to find out what. I was afraid, but I had to pull myself together and act as if nothing were wrong. I needed to focus on my goal, which was to get him to confess to killing my parents. He would be captured, and I would be saved. It was as easy as that, but we all know things are never as easy as they seem.

We started to drive. It was hard to keep myself upright with the hard turns he was making, and the constant motion was starting to make me feel queasy, so I laid down. We drove in silence, only the sound of the engine rolling through my ears.

It must have been an hour before he finally spoke to me, "You can come up front now."

I climbed to the front, landing in a captain's style chair. I looked to him and smirked.

"What?"

"Nothing. I'm just happy."

"Okay, good." He was silent again, but his face appeared to want to say something. After a paused he spoke again, "I've really missed you. How've they been treating you? Have they been total pricks like all fucking cops are?"

This was my time to show I was with him. "Yes! They've all been fucking assholes. Especially this bitch Janelle, she never leaves me the fuck alone. They all think I did it, so they keep treating me like I'm just some prisoner with special treatment being able to live in my own home. Like it's some big burden they have to be there watching me."

"You're too beautiful for prison."

"Thank you!" I smiled. "I feel the same way."

As we drove, we found ourselves bonding over different things we loved. It was strange to be doing that with my husband who was the murderer of my parents. Although I knew this wasn't real and I had a motive in getting him to feel more connected to me, I had to get him to confess. This was the way I figured it would happen. I had to build trust and when I felt the time was right, I would ask him.

Our time together was strange. It almost felt like a blur of days mixed into one. We were laughing together, singing to songs we heard on the radio and eating burgers on the road, but I soon noticed we barely ever stopped. We would pull over to use the restroom, grab a quick bite, it was always through a drive-thru, but we would never pull over to sleep. He was constantly snorting what I assumed to be cocaine and would have the energy again to keep driving.

The longer he didn't sleep, the scarier his driving became. I started to realize that if he was going to kill me at all, it would be on accident from our car going off the road.

"Hey, would you want me to drive for a bit so you can get some sleep?"

"Now why the fuck would I want you to do that?"

"Oh, I'm sorry, I just . . . "

"WHAT DO I ALWAYS TELL YOU ABOUT FUCKING APPOLOGIZING?"

There he was. The man I didn't know.

"I know. I know. I forgot. A beautiful woman should never have to apologize."

His rage calmed down, but my anxiety continued to rise, causing me to take deep breaths in through my nose and out through my mouth.

"Are you okay?" he asked.

"I think so. I just . . . don't feel very well."

"What's wrong? Do you need some water?"

"I'm fine. I'm just a little nauseous." As soon as I said the word, a flash hit me. I couldn't remember the last time I had started my period. "Oh, God."

"What now?"

"I think . . ." I looked to him, my entire life coming down in a crash as this nightmare would now live with me forever in the form of an innocent little baby. "I think I might be pregnant."

He pulled to the side of the road. "Are you fucking kidding?" He grinned. "Luke! Are you fucking kidding?" he asked louder.

I shook my head. "No."

"Luke! This is fantastic!"

"Wait! What? Why?"

"You didn't think I'd have another plan for the money, huh?"

"It's impossible. I'm on birth control."

"Oh, Luke. That face sure is beautiful, but what's behind it sure is dumb as shit."

The nightmare I was living was getting worse. I couldn't go on with myself knowing a piece of him would one day be out into the world, possibly doing this to someone else. I couldn't. I couldn't have this baby.

My insides were rattled with fear, disgust, and pure hatred for this man, and it was all my fault. He fooled me again and this time, I wouldn't even have been able to stop it. It was the time. I had to ask him. I had to ask him, or else I never would.

"Why did you murder my parents?"

He snorted. "You tell me the best news possible and then ask me why I murdered your parents? What kind of move it that?"

"I just want to know WHY YOU MURDERED MY PARENTS?" Something inside of me snapped. I threw myself onto him, my hands wrapping around his neck, squeezing as hard as I could. "YOU FUCKING BASTARD! I WANT YOU TO FUCKING DIE!" I squeezed and squeezed, my hands aching from the pressure I wasn't used to.

He pushed the gas, horns blaring from the cars passing by.

"Why? WHY?"

His voice croaked. "Get off of me, bitch!"

He was stronger than me. He pushed me back to my side of the van, slamming my back against the door. The knob to roll the window up and down bruising my spine.

"What the fuck are you doing, Luke? Are you working with them?"

I shook my head no, tears pouring down my face in streams that could fill a river.

"You want to fucking know why I killed your parents? YOU WANT TO FUCKING KNOW WHY?" His yell filled the van with thunderous roars. "Because the first time I saw your face on the cover of that magazine, I wanted to kill you . . ."

It all came out in blasts of howling sobs. "SO END IT."

The devilish grin plastered on his face was the last thing I saw before he slammed his foot on the gas, abruptly turning the steering wheel to the right, causing the van to fly over a cliff. My last words echoed through both of ours ears. "NO! THE BABY! THE BABY!"

Chapter Twenty

I shot up, sweat trickling down my neck, gasping for air.

"You dozed off for a while there."

I turned to meet his eyes in the rear-view mirror. Frightened, I didn't know where I was, but at the same time I did know. I was safe in the van.

"Must've been some dream. I could hear you moaning from up here." A devilish grin plastered his face. "Before you come up, look in the bag behind my seat. There's a wig in there. Put it on."

I couldn't believe I'd fallen asleep. I'd completely let my guard down in front of him, leaving myself defenseless with a murderer. My husband. The dream lingered with me. It felt so real, it was hard to shake what I had imagined, but I had to keep going. I had to continue to live because almost losing it all for that brief episode of slumber, made me realize I had much more to live for.

I took a moment to collect myself. I took deep breaths in and out before reaching into the bag finding the brunette wig Mitch had talked about. I pulled my hair up and put it on.

"You look beautiful as a brunette," he called from the front.

"Thank you." I met his eyes once more in the rear-view mirror as I made my way to the front. "May I please look in the mirror to see if I put it on correctly?" I asked him politely, trying to appease whatever version of him I was going to be getting, knowing he could instantly switch.

"Sure, but make it fast."

I made the minor adjustments needed and sat back in silence. "Mitch?" I closed the mirror and positioned myself towards him.

"Yeah?"

"Where are we going?"

"Up north."

"To Canada?"

"Yes."

"Oh, I love it there! I'm excited!" The false excitement was masking the sheer terror I still had from my dream.

"I have a friend who's going to help us get to Switzerland."

I reached my hand out to touch his arm. "I love that plan." I smiled before sitting back comfortably, trying to relax in the old, stained seat. "Let me know if you need me to drive so you can rest." Why had I said that? My dream flashed in my mind.

He snapped his head towards me, and I could tell he was questioning my motives.

"Mitch. This is it," I began to say. "This is what we wanted. To just be you and me, with no one in our ears saying we're doing something wrong. This is *our* life!" I smiled. "You and me. Together!" I reached for his hand, which was resting off of the arm rest. "I'm here with you. This is all I've ever known to be true. I love you more than you'll *ever* know, and I *trust* you. I know you'll protect me no matter what. I know that what you did, you did for *us*. So we could be together, happily, for the rest of our lives."

I squeezed his hand again, trying to convey with my eyes that I was there for him. That I wasn't going to ruin what we had going on. But I was lying with my eyes. I was telling him what he wanted to hear. This man. This stranger. My husband.

Somewhere over the past few weeks, I had grown stronger, even though I didn't feel like I had. I couldn't let the dream I had take focus away from what I was supposed to do. This entire ordeal had become more than just me. It had become something I had to do for my parents, for those two women and for anyone else Jason Feldstein had hurt in his life. It was all up to me. I was going to help get this man and I wasn't going to let my feelings of being afraid get in the way.

"I want us to be honest with each other. Can you do that? For me?" I asked him.

"What do you mean? What do you want to know?" His voice was tense.

"Well," I lingered. "Should I call you Mitch or Jason? I love both names, but I want to know which one *you* prefer."

He seemed a little shocked at the question. It was as if he knew he could only be one. The man who was his past or the man he created, although, either one would lead him down the same road.

I broke the silence when there wasn't an answer. "Is it alright if I call you Mitch? I'm just so used to it, and that's who I fell in love with."

"Mitch is fine."

"Okay, good."

There was silence while we drove, but this time, we were holding hands. I knew he wasn't the man I thought he was, but for that brief moment, it felt nice to have my hand held during the most traumatic experience I had ever been through even though he was the one putting me through it. The "pretending," as Janelle had told me to do, tricked me into feeling how nice it was to feel like the man I loved, loved me back. I could hear her voice repeating in my head, *pretend that you love him.* But all of the pretending, no matter how strong I thought I was, made it feel like I still loved him. And in a way, I still did.

Everything happened so quickly, there wasn't much time to process it all. I knew he wasn't who he was, but in the midst of losing my parents and my life, I had lost the man I loved. That was an odd feeling to have. The feeling of hating someone and loathing them, but yet, still being in love with the part of them that once made me so happy. It made what I knew I had to do hard, but easy in this weird mindfuck game of tug-o-war inside my head.

"Will you tell me what your childhood was like?" I asked softly, my voice almost a cracked whisper.

"Why are you acting different?" he shot back.

He could tell I was trying to get at him. He was smart, I'll give him that much.

"I'm not. I've just had a lot of time to think about you. About me. About us." I paused. "I love you and I want to know everything about you, Mitch. Don't you want to know everything about me? I mean we're in love and sharing a life together. It only makes sense I'd want to hear stories of little Mitch and where you grew up." I nervously smiled.

"You want to hear stories?" he asked in a harsh, abrasive tone. "I told you I was the bastard child the entire town looked down on. No one fucking liked me and always tried to kick my ass every chance they got. Imagine walking around town in piece of shit clothes with bruises all over your face from the assholes who made fun of you. No one fucking cared about me." He looked my way. "Is that what you wanted to hear? That I was never taken care of? That I had to fend for my-fucking-self most of the time? That my life was shit? Goddammit, Luke, it's always been. Until I met you."

"I'm glad you met me," I said, quietly. "I'm glad everything can be how you've always wanted it to be now."

"No, it's never going to be exactly how I want it to be because it got fucked up."

"How?"

"Because your fucking parents couldn't keep their noses out of our relationship. It wasn't their fucking business." I had unintentionally unleashed Jason. "As soon as I saw the picture of you on the cover of that magazine, I knew I had to have you. I had to have you *and* your money. I never thought anything would get in the way until it fucking did."

"Yeah, but they're gone now, so it shouldn't matter."

"And we're on the fucking run. That fucking matters."

"Well, we're together."

"The money. That's not with us." He paused. "I wanted you, but I wanted your money more. I wanted to marry you and live a happy, well-kempt life, with you on my arm, living as leisurely as I could in all of the best resorts in the world. *That's* the life I wanted. The life I fucking deserve. But when your parents started to snoop around and exposed me, my plan changed, and I knew I had to get rid of them. I'd done it before."

My eyes shot open. This was it; he was confessing.

I began listening intently to him. I felt like that's all I could do; sit there and wait for him to fully admit it. To just *say* the one thing I needed him to say, that he *murdered* my parents. This was the moment that was going to change everything. It would be the moment that would bring back some sort of normalcy in my life, whatever that was going to look like now. I was the only one in my family left. I had a legacy to fulfill, my parents' legacy, and I was never going to let their names be spoken with anything other than praise.

The silence after he spoke was the loudest silence I'd ever heard. It was deafening. "Mitch?"

"God, what is it, Luke?" he snapped.

"I love you. You know that, right? I've loved you since I first caught you staring at me . . . You saved me, you know? And I don't think I'll ever be able to repay you for that." I lingered on my words, trying to think of what to say next. "For me personally, you have no idea how you've changed my life. I don't think you'll ever actually know." I paused. "But before we go on and share our lives together, I just want to ask this once and then never bring it up again."

He looked over at me, full of disgust and agitation. "What?"

"Why did you do it?"

"Do what?"

I didn't want to look him in the eye, but I knew if I didn't, everything I was saying wouldn't sound genuine. It wouldn't sound believable. I had to gather whatever courage I had left and turn towards the man who took everything away from me.

As nonchalantly as I could, I said, "You know, murder my parents."

"You *know* why."

"Not truly. You've kind of brushed over it. 'They were in the way.' That's about it. Please, just tell me so I can process it and let it go."

He started to slow the van down, paying closer attention to me. "Why do you need to know that?"

"I just want to hear you say it once and then never again."

I jerked forward as he slammed the brakes. "What the fuck are you doing? Are you working with them?" He grabbed at my shirt, trying to rip it away from my chest. "Are you wearing a fucking wire?"

"No, Mitch. I'm not." I fought back, pushing his hands away. "Look at me," I said, then yelled, "LOOK AT ME! I just want to be able to move on from all of this shit and be with you. I just want *you*. Can't you see that?"

"You just want *me*? Is that it, huh?" he mocked.

"Yes." I looked at him, my eyes trying to tell him one thing when my heart and head were saying another.

His eyes made the narrowing expression that now frightened me.

"Mitch, shouldn't we keep going?" I gestured. "We're stopped in the middle of the freeway."

"If you want me so bad, then have me," he said, reaching for the back of my head, pulling it in towards his lap.

"Not here, Mitch," I said, my voice quiet, yet stern.

"Why?" he questioned. "No one's around. Prove you want me so badly."

My heartbeat began to quicken, my insides shaking uncontrollably and my breathing becoming more frantic. "I don't need to prove anything to you. Don't you trust me?"

He pushed on my resisting head harder.

"Mitch, no!"

"What did you say to me?" he questioned. "You *never* fucking tell me no." In his fit of rage, he grabbed my hair and pulled my head back before shoving my face back into his groin. Holding my head down firmly with one hand, he began to undo his pants with the other. All I could think about was how long I would have to endure this before I would be rescued. Every second felt like it was its own individual hour. And as frightened as I was, I wasn't going to let this happen.

Somehow, I found the strength to bring my hand up and started to punch as hard as I could, anywhere I could.

"You fucking bitch," he groaned, finally letting go of my head.

I scrambled to get upright and quickly opened the door, jumping out onto the dimly lit darkness of the open road and began to run. When I heard him start to come after me, I looked at my surroundings to see where we were. I had been asleep for most of the drive, so I had no idea where we could be. I only had a subconscious knowing that I was safe, or so I thought. My rescuers were nowhere in sight, and we were somewhere unfamiliar.

Chapter Twenty-One

The pitch black silence of the night filled the unknowing of my location with a sense of something terrible happening. Those could very well have been my last moments and that is exactly what it felt like. I was going to be killed, and I had no idea where I was or if someone would even find me.

Then, as if it were a sign from my parents, I heard the sound of crashing waves. All of a sudden, I knew exactly where I was. We were on the Bixby Bridge in Big Sur. I only recognized it in the dark because I'd been there once before with my parents. I was maybe eight years old at the time. We were at our home for a few weeks before we had to be back in New York for an opening, and my parents wanted to give me a history lesson. So, we drove to the bridge and took one of my most cherished photos of us together and we look so happy. It was like we were a normal family, and we weren't known by the entire world. So, to be in this place of a happy memory and not knowing if it was the end, seemed like being there was happening by something greater than myself.

I only had one option which was to run straight and follow the road.

I was running fast. As fast as my legs would take me. So fast that I could feel them disconnecting from my body, but all the while, taking me to my freedom.

I wasn't fast enough.

He grabbed my arm, my feet tripping over one another as he pushed me down. "YOU BITCH! Get up and get the fuck back into the van."

"NO!" I screamed. "SOMEBODY HELP ME! PLEASE! Help me." Tears streamed down my face as I stumbled to get up. The hold he had on my arm grew tighter as he began to drag me.

I was able to fight against him this time. Adrenaline filled me with strength. I tried moving my body, my arms, anything to get away from his grip. I began hitting him with my other hand trying to make him release me, but then he grabbed that one as well, pulling me up to him.

We were face to face, heavily breathing from the struggle we had given one another. I was still trying to fight, jolting my body this way and that. The dominance of his grip forced me to move back with him as he pushed me against the guard rail.

"You fucking want me, don't you, bitch?" He pushed me further, the top half of my body leaning slightly over the rail.

Through my cries, I pleaded with him, "Mitch, please! Please don't do this! I love you. I'm sorry. I'm so sorry. I just . . ."

"How many times do I have to fucking tell you? A beautiful woman should *never* have to fucking apologize." His grip somehow got even tighter around my arms, the feeling of a bruise I know was already forming.

"Please, Mitch! Please don't do this!" I cried. "We can figure this out. Please, let me go. You're hurting me. Please!"

The stinging on my cheek throbbed from the slap he placed upon it. The heat was rising as he placed his hand around my neck, slowly gripping it tighter. One of my arms was now free, but I stopped fighting back. I thought if I continued, he would push me over and that would be my end.

I gripped the edge of the guard rail as firmly as I could, staring him directly in his dark, dead eyes, holding my ground. Showing I wasn't afraid.

He released his other hand from my other arm and ripped my shirt open. "I fucking knew it." He gripped my neck tighter.

I started coughing from the pressure on my throat, barely able to get any air in, and I realized I should stay as calm as possible.

My breaths became shallow, and I was able to whisper, "Mitch, you don't have to do this."

"But Luke, I do. I *really* do," he snickered. "You lied to me. I can't be married to a woman who lies to me. Who do you think I am?"

That was the one question I honestly didn't know how to answer. I knew Mitch Bellamy. He was the kind, handsome man who loved me and wanted to spend the rest of his life with me. He was the man I adored and was madly in love with. This Jason person was a stranger to me, and I had no idea what he was truly capable of. Besides, *he* was the one who *lied* to me. Although I didn't want to, I knew I had to continue to play victim to his erratic, domineering behavior. I wanted to shut down and continue to scream out for help. I just wanted someone to hear me. I didn't care who, I just needed someone, *anyone*.

He slowly inched his face towards mine, having the nerve to kiss me. "You don't want to keep making me angry now, do you?" I shook my head no. "Good girl. Let's get back in the van and keep driving. Do you understand me?" I didn't answer right away, so he tightened his grip, cutting off more oxygen. "I asked you a question."

I shook my head vigorously yes.

"Good." He released his hand and started to push me towards the van, holding my arms behind my back.

My rescuers were nowhere in sight. Janelle had promised me nothing bad would happen, but it seemed like the only person I could trust to get out of this was myself. I started to think about every book I'd ever read. Trying to remember if there was any scene that could help me think of what to do, but my mind was getting lost in thinking it was all going to end. I wouldn't have a next chapter.

My mind had grown completely blank. I had been so naïve to the real world that I only knew a fictional one where I wasn't prepared for any type of danger that could come my way. I had been privileged, selfish and unconcerned about real people and what could actually go on in someone's life. There, in one of the worst moments of my life, I realized how I could do something to help others who found themselves in a similar situation. Where a partner was abusive both mentally and physically, even deadly. I had the resources to help, but before I was able to help others, other women, I had to help myself.

With quick thinking, I stuck my leg out tripping Mitch behind me. His grip around my arms released freeing me to make my next move. I ran back towards the guard rail, not really knowing what my next move would be until he caught up to me.

I quickly spun around with as much force as I was able to

will, taking a swing at his face. The surprised hit caused him to buckle, and I was able to sneak past his reaching arm, pushing him over the side. A calmness fell over me as the waves crashed in the distance, and I heard the sound of his death.

Chapter Twenty-Two

"Luke, I'm so sorry we didn't get here faster." Janelle bent down to console me as I sat, holding my legs in towards my chest, crying into my knees as I rocked myself back and forth. "You did it, Luke. You got him."

I was shaking too much to be able to get any words out. "Why . . . weren't . . . you . . . here?" I managed to say between sobs.

"We were trying to stay at a safe distance, for your safety. I'm sorry, Luke. That's all I can say, but you did it, Luke! You got him!"

"No, I killed him. He made me just like him."

"No, Luke. You aren't anything like him at all. It was self-defense. We have it all on tape."

"But he didn't even say he killed my parents."

"Yeah, but we have enough. And," she paused, "We have you saying no. That's the important thing. We have him threatening and attacking you on tape." She put an arm around me, trying to reassure how everything was okay. "Luke, don't let yourself feel like that. Listen, you helped catch someone the FBI has been looking for, for a while.

Sure, we would've loved to have had him behind bars and tried, but at least now he can't hurt anyone else ever again."

I scoffed. "He'll be hurting me for the rest of my life."

Janelle looked at me, knowing I was right. Mitch would always be attached to everything I did. He would be a constant staple of how one mistake could change the whole trajectory of your life. He wasn't going to be a person I could easily forget about. He was going to be the *only* person I was going to think about *every single day* for the rest of my life. He was the *one* person I loved more than anything at one point, and the *one* person who took *everything* away from me in an instant. He would be in my life, in my mind, until the day I died because every time I thought about my parents, I'd think about him.

The FBI brought me back home, where I then had to go through every detail of what had happened with Mitch. Though, all I wanted to do was go to sleep and wake up from what felt like a nightmare.

People were still outside of our property, yelling things and calling me names. They didn't know. They didn't know what I had endured in the past few months of knowing a man I innocently fell in love with. They didn't know the pain, the torture or the manipulation that was put on me. They didn't know what I'd have to live with for the rest of my life. They didn't know I'd just killed a man. All they thought was how it was my fault my beloved parents were dead. Yes, it *was* my fault and it's something I'm going to have to live with for the rest of my life. It's also something I need to embrace and take on knowing I had to do what I did to catch the guy who started it all and taking his life in the process.

I took someone's life, even if it wasn't in vein, as a way to serve justice for my parents. As a way to protect myself from whatever he would've done to me, which would have been *exactly* what I did to him.

"What's going to happen to me?"

"Ms. Townsend," Agent Kai began, "You're going to have a clean slate. We have it on tape that he was attacking you. We know you didn't intentionally push him over the guard rail. You were defending yourself. We know that."

"What about everything else?"

"We're going to have a press conference explaining the situation and how you helped the FBI track down and obtain Mr. Feldstein. We'll let them know there was an altercation which ended in the demise of his life." Agent Kai looked to Agent Whitmore and nodded.

"We're hoping you can get back to a normal life now, Ms. Townsend. There's probably going to be some interviews the media are going to want to do with you. We'll brief you on all of those and have someone help you say exactly what should be said. Ultimately, you'll get back to your normal life and move on from all of this," Agent Whitmore added.

I started to laugh. "You think it's really going to be that easy, huh?" I looked at the two of them. "I mean, come on, the entire world hates me. It's not because I've lived a life not everyone gets to live, but they think *I killed my parents*. They have a reason to hate me *even more* now and I'm just supposed to do a couple of interviews, wash my hands like nothing ever happened? Come on! Coming back from this is going to be worse than living through it."

They knew I was right. They would be able to make my life look perfect on paper again, but they could never fix what I would actually have to live with.

Just then, the door burst open and Remy walked in,

bringing a light of hope with him. "Luke!" he cried, embracing me in a tight hug. "God, Luke, I'm so happy you're safe and this is all over."

"Where's Margot and Franklin?"

"They're on their way. I was closer, so I came straight over once they said I could."

I smiled at my friend, trying to show how much I appreciated him being there, but fully aware he had *no idea* what I had just gone through. He would never know the extent of how much my life had changed. It would never be the same again. *I* would never be the same again. I would never be the girl he once knew.

"Once everything gets cleared up, we should get out of here for a while and go on vacation somewhere. We'll lay out by the beach, eat amazing food, and go shopping! It'll be like a reset of your life," he emphasized.

I smiled at him again, knowing he was right in getting away for a while and distancing myself from what I knew would be an overwhelming period of time. But how could I just reset my life? I still had to bury my parents, figure out what I was going to do with the house and then figure out who I was going to be. I didn't want to be who I once was. Life seemed to have more meaning and more purpose now that I had experienced a trauma some women live with every day. "Yeah, that sounds nice."

And as if right on cue, Margot barged through the door in her extravagant way not caring to read the room or situation at hand with Franklin following behind. "Luke!" She embraced me in a hug. "Oh, Luke! I'm so happy you're okay. We heard what happened last night. You must be so scared and shaken up."

"Yeah, it was . . . . . . interesting."

"Well, I don't think that's the word I would use. But still, I'm so glad you're okay."

"Thanks Margot."

"Yeah, Luke, I don't know what we would've done if something happened to you."

"Thanks, Franklin."

"Okay, let's just tone down the emotions here," Remy said. "She just went through the most traumatic experience of her life. Let's give her some space to breathe for a second." He looked between the two of them. "We decided we're going to go on a vacay to get her away from here."

"I love that idea!" Margot exclaimed.

"Me too!" Franklin added. "Where should we go? Morocco? Dubai? Monte Carlo? Or maybe even Italy?" His eyes lit up.

They were too much for me. There was once a time when all of those places sounded like a party waiting to happen and I knew I'd have the *best* time in the world being there with people I enjoyed being around. But now, the idea of those glamorized places didn't spark any type of excitement within me whatsoever. I just wanted the press conference to happen so I could give my parents the sendoff they deserved. Then I would figure it out from there.

I would figure out who *I* was going to be.

Chapter Twenty-Three

As I was told, the media started to bombard me with calls. I had to turn off my phone because it wouldn't stop ringing day in and day out. I know people wanted to hear it from me directly, but I wasn't ready to face anyone. I needed a little bit of time which sounds contradictory of me wanting it all to be over. I was scared no one would believe me.

The FBI had agents stationed around the property 24/7, which provided a sense of safety, but I still felt like a prisoner in my own home. I couldn't so much as open my front door without one of them being there with a loaded gun in hand. Not that it bothered me, I felt protected. It was a surreal feeling of knowing that one day I might not be safe, and no one would be there to protect me. So, feeling trapped had made the world seem a little more frightening not knowing what would happen next.

I was all anyone could talk about. How could I not be? I was a spoiled, privileged, "rich girl." How could I be so naïve as to fall for a malicious psychopath who wanted me for my money? And in doing so, he killed my parents.

Agents Kai and Whitmore sent in a psychiatrist to talk to me twice a day. It helped, but she knew it would take more than her and a few sessions to get over what happened. It would probably take months, years even. Or I may *never* get over it. Watching your parents get brutally slain in front of you while being tied up isn't something you could ever easily forget. It was on repeat every time I closed my eyes. She prescribed me sleeping pills which helped, but it was still the last thing I thought about before falling asleep and the first thing I thought about every time I woke up. I was given exercises to do to come up with happier things to think about whenever those thoughts entered my mind. But again, it's not something that can easily be forgotten and that was just for the things regarding my parents. There was still everything that had happened to me personally.

A prep team came in to help advise me on how to answer questions pertaining to the sit-down interview I agreed to do. It was a 20/20 special with Diane Sawyer. It was the only interview I agreed to do because it made me comfortable as she was someone I knew because she was close friends with my parents. She would be the perfect person to tell my story to. Although I had been prepped by experts from the FBI, I still felt like I had an advantage, or the upper hand in helping people. I was coached on what to say about Mitch and who he was and how he came into my life. I was also a victim of domestic abuse and violence, who had a platform that could possibly help someone in the same, or similar, situation. So, I did what I thought was the right thing and I answered honestly.

"Tell us what happened. How could you not know Jason, or Mitch as he was known to you, was a bad guy? Is it alright if I call him by his name?"

"It's okay, I don't mind. I'm not going to allow myself to get triggered by his name. But umm . . ."

"Do you feel naïve, like you got tricked? Because I feel like, maybe in a sense, you did after hearing everything that happened from the very beginning."

"Well, to put it simply, I fell in love. That's really it. I met a handsome, charming man who treated me how anyone would want to be treated by the person they love. He never showed me anything *but* that love. There wasn't anything else to elude to even the slightest hint of what my parents and friends saw in him."

"Would you say you were blinded by love?"

"Although I hate the term, yes. I was and I now know that's a real thing that happens to people. You hear it as a teenager or see it in movies, or even read it in books. Though it never really seems like it could be real. Not many people know this about me, but I'm a very well-read person. So, that's something I only ever rolled my eyes to or scoffed at because, like it would happen to me, right?! I've always thought I was untouchable. I know that's a very small minded, ignorant way of thinking, but that's who I was before everything happened. I was selfish, self-centered and only cared about myself and how *I* was feeling. I never could've imagined, in any of my wildest dreams or imaginations of the written word, that I would *ever* find myself in this position where my naivety was taken advantage of. That naivety made me lose everything."

"What are your plans now, for the future? I mean, you helped the FBI catch someone on their most wanted list and the truth of what really happened is out. Your name is cleared. Do you plan on resuming the life you lived before? Are we going to see you on the covers of tabloids every week? Traveling the world? Partying?"

"I think a lot of people would want to see that. To see that I haven't changed. That I'm still the person who doesn't care about the world around her, but I'm not that girl anymore. That girl died the second my parents were taken from me."

"Luke you don't . . . . . ."

"No, it's okay. I want to tell the truth and I don't care how it makes me look," I paused. "A part of me died watching my parents be taken from me. I don't know if I'll ever get over that. It's something I live with every day and see every time I close my eyes. I've been working with a psychiatrist, but it's just something that's going to take time, patience and strength to come to terms with. It's not something I'll ever get over. It's something I'll never get to *un-see*. To answer your question though, my plan now is to utilize the resources I have and make a foundation in my parents' name to help women who are being abused by their partners. My goal is to help them in all aspects of starting their lives over and getting back to being as normal as possible, whatever that may be, because that's what they deserve. I've already built a fantastic team around me and we're working with other foundations to help these women. We're going to offer everything to these strong, beautiful women from housing, to legal services, even therapy to help get over, or manage the trauma they've endured. We're going to provide an easy number that can be called or even texted. We will even pick them and their children up, no matter what time of night, and get them to safety. I just want to help in any way I can because there are so many women out there who have had, or currently have, it far worse than I did who have suffered longer. I was lucky, in a sense, because I didn't have to fight my way out. I was going to be saved either way. I can't be the person I used be with what I've gone through now. One, it wouldn't feel right and two, there's so many more important things in the world than what designer bag I can buy next. That's obnoxious to me now, to think that once upon a time that was all I cared about when there are women out there who need help and *I* can help them. It's going to be as my parents would say, 'My greatest creation.' This foundation, in their name, so I can help women who need it."

The End

Acknowledgments

The first thank you goes to my husband. Your unwavering support and belief in me never goes unnoticed. Thank you for pushing me to keep going even when I felt like I wasn't good enough.

To my beautiful children, I hope mommy is making you proud and showing you that it's possible for your dreams to come true.

Emi, my incredible editor, you have once again made one of my dreams possible. Thank you for being so encouraging and offering your brilliant mind to helping indie authors like myself. I will forever be grateful for having you in my life! I can't wait to send you the next one!

Deanna, you are one incredible human. You have supported me and every other indie author with such passion, excitement and genuine love. You are truly appreciated more than you will ever know! I love you sister!

Camarin, my greatest friend. Thank you for everything you have done for Luke and her story. You have been my biggest hype girl since we met. Thank you for listening when I needed to vent and for offering your kindness always. I truly value your friendship.

Nikki, my bestie!!! Thank you for being such a wonderful friend! Thank you for believing in me and for liking the same things I do. One day I hope to meet you in person so we can just hang out, talk and laugh because I know together we would be a riot!

My final thank you goes to you, the reader, for taking a chance on an indie author who is trying to make her dream career happen one story at a time. I hope you were able to see Luke's story like a little movie playing in your beautiful mind. I also hope you felt as if you were sitting around having a chat with a friend who was telling you about something that happened to her. Truly, thank you for reading this as it's always very nerve-wracking to put your work out there for people to read. So, thank you. I very grateful for you.

Please leave a review on Amazon, Good Reads, Barnes & Noble, etc. as reviews really help Indie Authors!

Instagram: @BrittRoth_Author

TikTok: @BrittRoth_Author

www.brittrothauthor.com

About the Author

Brittany resides in Southern California with her husband, two children and three dogs. She still views her life as a musical, but over the past year her harshest critics have now become a part of her ensemble.

When she isn't being a wife and mom she loves to… who is she kidding?! That's a full time job.

She is a sandwich enthusiast who is ALWAYS on the hunt for the Most Delicious Sandwich Ever!!! She rue's the day she turned down ordering a steak sandwich, which was the special of the day, only to have one, *tiny* bite of her husband's. It was the MOST DELICIOUS sandwich she's ever had. She even went back the following week to order it, but they had no idea what she was talking about. That delicious bite has haunted her ever since. One day she hopes to come into contact with a sandwich that can uphold to that level of perfection.

www.ingramcontent.com/pod-product-compliance
Lightning Source LLC
Chambersburg PA
CBHW061538310726
48972CB00008B/2506